McElroy turned his head to look into the passageway. It was not easy; wedged in as he was between the jutting stones, he was forced to move carefully to avoid scraping the skin off his cheek. Then he saw what Cracchiolo was staring at. Out in the passageway, hanging in the blackness twenty paces from where he stood, were a swarm of glowing coals. He looked closer and suddenly knew what they were. His stomach knotted.

The glowing coals were eyes.

THE TARTARUS INCIDENT

WILLIAM GREENLEAF

ACE SCIENCE FICTION BOOKS
NEW YORK

THE TARTARUS INCIDENT

An Ace Science Fiction Book / published by arrangement with
the author

PRINTING HISTORY
Ace edition / May 1983

Copyright © 1983 by William Greenleaf
Cover art by James Gurney
 For information address: Ace Science Fiction Books,
200 Madison Avenue, New York, New York 10016

ISBN: 0-441-79846-2

Ace Science Fiction Books are published by Charter Communications, Inc.,
200 Madison Avenue, New York, N.Y. 10016.
PRINTED IN THE UNITED STATES OF AMERICA

For my parents
JOSEPH AND SHIRLEY GREENLEAF
with love and respect

Tartarus: *1) in ancient Terran mythology, the level of Hades reserved for punishment of the worst offenders; 2) a semideveloped planet of the Omega Centauri Sector, landed by J. Bannat on 31.97 GCC; best known for the series of events often referred to as The Tartarus Incident. (see McElroy, Oliver; Omega Centauri Sector, history of exploration and development; Audit Agency archives—General Services Administration)*

—Third Oxford Macropedia,
UNSA (fourteenth) edition

PROLOGUE

"Hey, Gordie. We got a problem."

Gordie Turner was halfway through the narrow passageway that separated *Graywand*'s service bays from the third-level receiving dock when Josk Cooper's words stopped him. He turned and saw Cooper limping toward him, waving a yellow sheet of paper in one grimy hand.

"Rehfield's pod," Cooper puffed as he reached Gordie and thrust the repair order toward him. "Looks like a blown circuit in the drive control system."

Gordie's eyes flicked briefly to the repair order, but he made no move to take it. "Too bad, Coop. I got a date tonight. Find someone else."

"Too bad for you, kid." Cooper was chief engineer in *Graywand*'s small-vessel repair shop. He was as scrawny as a bird's claw, with a built-in stoop and a pocked face stretched tight over a grinning skull. He spoke with a nasal twang that set Gordie's teeth on edge. "Rehfield's making a skip tomorrow. Wants his machine fixed now." Cooper

2

made an elaborate show of looking around at the empty service bays. "Looks like you're the only one left, kid. Bad luck. A bit late getting away, eh?"

"C'mon, Coop." Gordie had worked late because Cooper had asked him to finish a stator-motor rebuild that evening. He had not done so by choice—a fact Cooper knew as well as he. "Give Rehfield a pod from the pool."

Cooper shook his head, chuckling at some inner amusement. "Tried to, but he wouldn't have it. Said he don't trust the pool pods. Old Rehfield, he's a real individual." The chuckle turned into a choking cough that wracked his skeletal frame and produced a large glob of greenish phlegm, which he deposited noisily on the graymetal deck beside Gordie's foot. He cleared his throat, hawked up another glob, and placed it neatly beside the first.

"I worked last night, Coop—"

"Life's a real pain sometimes," Cooper admitted without much sympathy. He reached across and stuffed the repair order into the breast pocket of Gordie's coveralls. "Get to it, kid. Oughtn't take more'n an hour."

"I don't *have* an hour," Gordie pleaded, but Cooper had already turned to shuffle toward the service elevator that would take him to the living quarters several levels above.

Gordie made a sound that was not exactly a word. He yanked the repair order from his pocket—tearing it nearly in two but caring not the least—and cursed as he struggled with Rehfield's nearly illegible scrawl. Rehfield had gotten an amber warning signal during his last skip—failure in the spud's tertiary connectors, if Rehfield could be trusted to read the signals correctly. Which was doubtful, Gordie told himself bitterly—Rehfield was in the Audit Agency, and how much could an accountant know about operating a pod? It was impossible to say what he might find in the circuitry. Maybe a short in the wiring harness or maybe a blown drive engine. You could never tell about those worn-out old pods they gave the Audit Agency.

"Who is she?"

. Gordie's head jerked up. Cooper had stopped halfway across the garage. His face was split by a leering grin that added to its already cadaverous look. "Your date, kid. Who is she?"

"Forget it, Coop."

"C'mon, kid. You can tell me."

Gordie glared across at Cooper, teeth clenched. Then his shoulders slumped in resignation. "Camilla di Pierro."

Cooper's eyebrows lifted. "Camilla. Oh, you poor, poor boy." He jabbed a bony finger at Gordie. "Hurry it up, boy. Maybe she'll keep it warm for you." Cackling lewdly, he shuffled away toward the elevator.

What a jerk, thought Gordie.

Graywand's small-vessel repair shop was a vast open cavern occupying three levels of the ship's stern. Two hundred service bays, each with its own supply of diagnostic and repair tools, were arranged in tidy rows, separated by wide aisles. A central parts store and tool crib supported all three levels. It was not a cheerful place: graymetal walls with bare seams, stark overhead lighting, odors of dirt and lubricant. It was a place of functional efficiency, a place where men and machines came together intimately to sort out their mutual problems.

The dirty-gray sameness of the shop carried over to the vehicles that were serviced there. Except for minor design variations, each pod was much like the other: a graymetal box three meters by four squatting on four stabilizer pads, a single gullwing door, and an efficient design of rounded corners and smooth surfaces. And all the character of a turnip.

Rehfield, in an effort to make his pod different from the others, had proclaimed it the *jack-a-dandy* in bright orange letters splashed across its stubby nose. Gordie found it after a long search (*why can't these jerks take a minute to jot down the service bay numbers on the repair orders?*) far back against the outer wall of the second level. He was nervous and jittery—thinking of Camilla, conscious of time ticking away—by the time he'd unbolted the pod's control chair and moved it out of the way, squirmed into the workspace under the console, and began removing the lower panel.

The control circuits for every electrical system in the pod originated in the control pad, then led down into the inner workings of the console, where they were organized into functioning units and distributed to the various components. Since *jack-a-dandy* was an old pod, built when actual wiring harnesses were used in backup systems, Gordie decided that the most likely place for circuit failure was in the harness just inside the console's lower panel, where sharp metal edges sometimes cut through the fiber insulation.

He was beginning to feel better as the first of the retaining bolts came away in his hand. He knew his way around the innards of these old pods; with luck he would be able to locate the fault and get it fixed in time to meet Camilla for a drink in the Cornucopia and a romp in his little cubicle on the eighth level. Maybe a late dinner afterward, then another romp. His blood ran a few degrees warmer; his fingers worked more quickly at the bolts. Ah, Camilla. . . .

The panel dropped away. Gordie looked up into the console and felt his mouth dry up and his luck run out. The shiver of lustful anticipation turned into a shudder of revulsion.

The wiring circuits inside the console were a mess. Cables that should have been neatly banded by control function hung instead in hopeless tangles. An obscene, greenish-white crust of corrosion covered every exposed connection. The metal sides of the compartment were covered with what looked to be a combination of scaly rust and green slime.

Gordie groaned. He'd seen similar conditions in other pods which, like *jack-a-dandy*, had been made before the designers realized that prudence required placement of the water tank somewhere other than adjacent to the console, where dampness could react with the sensitive control system components. But he had never seen it this bad. Sometime in the past the tank had leaked through to the compartment. Someone had gone in and fixed it—someone who had sealed the tank but had not taken the time to repair the damage it had left. So Gordie Turner, who always drew the short straw, who wouldn't even be here but for the simple fact that he was the last one getting out of the shop, born-loser Gordie Turner was going to have to dig into that mess and find the single connection, out of dozens, that had given up the struggle against corrosion.

His despair deepened as he realized that an even more dreadful problem lurked there in the console. The wiring harnesses were a shambles, one massive circuit failure waiting to happen, waiting for Gordie Turner to stick his big fingers in and upset the delicate balance that separated the entire system from breakdown. It would all have to be ripped out and replaced. Every circuit, every wire, every connector. Three hours work, minimum.

Camilla di Pierro would definitely not keep it warm for him. All because of Rehfield and his unreasonable insistence that his precious pod be repaired tonight. There was no reason, Gordie fumed, why Rehfield couldn't take a pod from the common pool. No reason at all. He would certainly draw one in better condition than this old junker.

Gordie licked his lips, wondering if it were true that, once stood up, Camilla never offered another chance. He lay on his back for a long time looking up at the tangle of wiring, thinking of Camilla and Rehfield, his mood wavering between bitterness and hopelessness—and somewhere in the back of his restless mind an idea began to form.

A way out.

As service techs went, Gordie Turner was a cut above the average. He liked working with machines; he believed in Josk Cooper's oft-spoken adage that if you were going to do a job, do it right. But Gordie was also a full-blooded male, stationed on *Graywand*, where the male population outnumbered the female by three to one. Which was why he was considering how he might take a shortcut in the repair of Rehfield's pod.

He worked through it slowly in his mind, feeling it out. The spud—a term commonly used for the k-stream commutator, shortened to k-tator and finally to spud—was the heart of the drive system, the fist-sized gadget behind the console that translated power from the drive engines into passage through the Kohlmann stream. In older pods like *jack-a-dandy*, built before the more sophisticated drive system was developed with its elaborate failsafe, the circuits connecting the spud to the drive engines were the single source of the rare but occasional drive system malfunction during breakout. By their nature, the drive engines were not subject to catastrophic failure. They either worked properly or they didn't work at all. The spud was similarly foolproof. As long as gravitational laws remained fixed, so did the k-stream functions of the spud and drive engines. But the connecting circuitry was subject to failure, and the best way to avoid drive system problems was to provide multiple options in that weak link. Triple backups were therefore installed in the circuitry of all pods. The primary circuit was a standard printed board, but secondary and tertiary circuits were hard-wired for maximum resistance to shock or electrical surge.

The amber light on *jack-a-dandy*'s console warned that the tertiary circuit had failed. Gordie Turner didn't see that as anything to get too worked up about. It did mean that if primary and secondary circuits also failed, the spud's connection with the drive engines would be lost; and if that happened during breakout, the results could be disastrous—*jack-a-dandy* and its crew would most likely be strung out through the k-stream with a combined density of something like one atom per hundred million kilometers. But Gordie had never heard of even a primary circuit failing during breakout. The odds against primary *and* secondary circuits failing simultaneously were—well, Gordie decided that the odds were too small even to consider.

Gordie wriggled out of the space under the console,

popped the crick out of his back, and found *jack-a-dandy*'s duty book in its niche beside the control pad. Rehfield was due for a two-week audit on a planet—Gordie could not pronounce a name that had r-b-d-t as its first four letters—in the Malachi Sector. After that the pod was scheduled for a routine service check.

Gordie licked his lips, thinking again of Camilla. A man couldn't pass up a chance with Camilla. He just couldn't. He snapped the duty book shut, returned it to its compartment, and got to work.

He went first to the stores area on the second level and withdrew a length of 7-x cable. Then he selected a few simple hand tools, returned to the pod, and squirmed into the cramped workspace under the console. It took only a few minutes to attach the cable to the base of the console, feed it down through the lower compartment, and attach the other end to the metal contact on the spud's housing. He replaced the panel, crossed his fingers, and gave power to the console.

The warning light above the control pad remained dark. He licked his lips again. Nobody will ever know, he told himself. Not even Josk Cooper.

Despite the nag of conscience, Gordie felt clever. He had accomplished his simple miracle by fooling the pod's brain into thinking the backup system was whole again. It wasn't, of course; the 7-x cable did not make the necessary connection between the spud and the drive engines, but instead merely linked the spud to the control pad. Not a valid connection by any means, not enough to make the circuit functional. But enough to quench the amber light, enough to get Gordie Turner out of the repair shop in time to meet Camilla.

He put his tools away and washed up quickly, thinking through the rest of his plan. He had it all worked out. When *jack-a-dandy* came in for its regular service, he would sneak in after hours and fix up the circuit the right way. In fact, he decided expansively as he scrubbed at the dirt under his fingernails, he would replace the gummed-up mess under the console with all new circuits. Rehfield would never have another problem with the old junkbucket.

He tossed the shop towel into the disposal bin and hurried toward the elevator without giving *jack-a-dandy* another glance.

As events transpired, Gordie would have fared better in the shop with *jack-a-dandy* that evening. His date with Camilla was a disaster. Her magnificent body was more than offset by a giggly personality and a way of saying "Oh, you!" that wore Gordie's nerves to a frazzle. She drank too much of the Cornucopia's icy white wine, fell asleep five minutes after Gordie steered her into his eighth-level cubbyhole, and was messily sick the next morning.

Gordie's other plans were also doomed by circumstance. When Rehfield's pod came in for its service check two weeks later, Gordie was stranded on a hellhole planet in the Brissom Range, making an emergency repair on a rangefinder pak in a Field Recon pod. The mechanic who performed the work on *jack-a-dandy* ran the standard stress tests without detecting Gordie's cable, and although formal procedure called for visual inspection of the control system circuitry during routine service checks, the procedure was rarely followed and the mechanic decided to skip it. Gordie made a mental note to watch for *jack-a-dandy*'s next scheduled service, but time and events intervened and he forgot.

Rehfield was eventually transferred to another sector of Omega, and Oliver McElroy, also with the Audit Agency, inherited *jack-a-dandy*. Shortly thereafter, Gordie was transferred to *Quinquilla*, and a year later joined a private mining firm and left to find his fortune in an unexplored region of Omega.

Three years later Vito Cracchiolo found Gordie's 7-x cable under unfortunate circumstances, and the Tartarus incident was written into Omega history.

CHAPTER ONE

Tom Stone was the last one in, still tucking shirttails into baggy brown trousers as he made his way through the hatchway six minutes before breakout and collapsed with a grunt into the corner chair. He surveyed the others with a bleary-eyed glance: Oliver McElroy working at the console; John Wheeler hunched over the counter, leafing through a file report; Vikki Redford and Vito Cracchiolo arguing their way through final supplies check. None of this was of particular interest to Stone, who had a thumping hangover from too much *sake* the night before. He leaned his head back and closed his eyes as *jack-a-dandy*'s hatchcover thumped into place with a whoosh of vented air.

"Glad you could join us," McElroy remarked without taking his eyes from the console readout screen.

Stone made an unintelligible grunt and slumped down in the chair, hands folded across his broad stomach.

McElroy shook his head at Stone's seeming inability to

11

learn from experience. He entered a command and watched the figures build across the readout screen in long, luminous lines as *jack-a-dandy*'s brain worked through the final coordination tests. He glanced at the chronometer above the console. Just under five minutes to breakout. Behind him, the argument between Vikki Redford and Vito Cracchiolo began heating up.

"You're nuts, Crackers." Vikki wasn't yelling yet, but she was close to it. "Not one person in ten makes it into Field Recon. The standards are too tough. They have to be."

"Sure they are." Cracchiolo kept his voice low, conscious of McElroy's need for concentration. He also kept it pitched at that placating tone that infuriated Vikki. "That's why half the people in Field Recon bought their way in. If you don't have the brains for it, all you need is the cash."

McElroy tapped *jack-a-dandy*'s destination coordinates into the cluster of keys that comprised the right half of the control pad and watched as a row of tiny numbers crept in single file across the screen. They hung for a moment against the black void, then vanished to be replaced by: READY FOR CROSS-PROOF. He reached forward and nudged the commbox switch. "Crew AA75D. McElroy and four. Destination 3RX-99301."

The *Graywand* commclerk responded promptly, his voice fuzzy as it came through the palm-size plate of the commbox. "Audit crew 75D, McElroy. Coordinates 3RX-99301 confirmed and set. Target Sierra. Please proceed with coordination proof."

McElroy once again entered the Sierra coordinates through the control pad. Behind him Vikki's voice rose in a brief moment of anger, then subsided.

"Set." McElroy pressed the enter key and waited while *jack-a-dandy*'s brain took a moment to consider what it had been told. Then the confirmation flashed across the screen, all in green:

COORDINATES SET—3RX-99301
CONFIRMED UNIT IDENT 1334-01-2009
AUTHORIZATION AFFIRMED—PRIORITY ORANGE
HOURS—72.20 GRAYWAND CONSTANT
READY . . .

"Confirmed," McElroy said into the commbox.

"Agreed," replied the commclerk. The check and doublecheck procedure, nuisance though it was, was a necessary safeguard. A k-stream skip represented a mutual effort between the navigation computers of the base vessel—in this case *Graywand*—and the pod's own brain and drive system. A k-stream skip was also an incredibly complex series of maneuvers that left no room for error. McElroy and the commclerk had received identical messages of confirmation, assuring them that *jack-a-dandy*'s brain and *Graywand*'s navigation computers had determined jointly that the target coordinates were properly set for the planet called Sierra.

"Sequences activated." McElroy pressed another control on the board, and the row of lights above the readout screen winked green. Drive engines were calibrated and set. "And confirmed."

"Where do you get that?" Vikki demanded loudly of Cracchiolo. "You have to get past a high-level review board for Field Recon. Are you saying the entire board can be bought off?"

"It doesn't take the whole board, Vikki. Just most of them."

"Full crew ident, please," said the commclerk.

McElroy's thumb had gone to the commbox switch, ready to break the connection. Now he drew it back, irritated. Just his luck to get a commclerk that went by the book. Clemens, probably. Snotty-nosed kid. Any other commclerk would have accepted McElroy's shortcut version of crew identification. He leaned forward to the commbox and spoke loudly against a fresh eruption from Vikki Redford. "Audit Manager, Oliver McElroy; Field

Senior, Tom Stone; assisting are Vito Cracchiolo, Vikki Redford, John Wheeler.''

A reply from the commclerk was lost under a blast from Vikki to the effect that, if it were so easy to get into Field Recon, why didn't Cracchiolo do it himself?

McElroy half-turned in his chair and snapped, ''Hold it down, you two.''

''Sure, cap'n,'' said Cracchiolo. ''Sorry.''

''I'll tell you something, Crackers,'' Vikki said, her voice only slightly less strident than before. ''I'm going to get into Field Recon, and I'm not buying my way in.''

''You think you can make it any other way?''

''Say again,'' McElroy said into the commbox.

''Audit Assistant Vito. Say again on surname, please.''

This could almost be funny, McElroy thought grimly. Almost. Behind him, Vikki recovered from the stunned silence provoked by Cracchiolo's last remark and exploded anew. McElroy sighed and leaned toward the black commbox plate. ''Who is this?''

''Lars Clemens, sir.''

''Got your roster, Clemens?''

''Yes, sir—''

''You'll find Cracchiolo's name in the Cs.''

After a moment's hesitation: ''Thank you, sir.''

''There's one other thing I want to point out,'' McElroy continued. ''Or perhaps you've already noticed that we have only forty-five seconds to breakout.''

Another brief pause. ''Right, sir. You are cleared for schedule. Coordinates are locked.''

''Thank you, Mr. Clemens. McElroy out.''

McElroy's fingers moved rapidly over the keyboard, entering the series of commands that gave *jack-a-dandy*'s drive system the authority to make the skip as directed. The screen rippled with a cascade of information, most of which he ignored. When it flashed SEQUENCE READY, he leaned back in the control chair and glanced up at the chronometer.

''Ten seconds,'' he said.

"—because I'm good," Vikki stormed. "I don't have to *buy* my way into anything. I can make it on my own. And I'll tell you something else, Cracchiolo—"

"Five seconds."

"—within five years I'll be in the Blue. I know that's too much for your Neanderthal mentality to grasp, but—"

There was a moment of drunk-stagger vertigo when the drive engines caught the signal from the spud and yanked them through the k-stream to the planet called Sierra. It happened with every skip, as if for a brief moment the pod was suspended between the gravity field of *Graywand* and the real gravity of the target planet. For that brief instant McElroy felt as if someone had dealt him a swift kick to the stomach that brought no pain but only the numbing loss of breath one would expect from a kick like that. The k-stream techs said that was nonsense. They insisted the moment of vertigo could not exist, for the simple reason that the Kohlmann stream provided no room for it. The pod existed in *Graywand*'s departure dock, then the stream was altered and the pod immediately existed on the target planet. There was no in-between, no such thing as travel time through the stream; and this meant that the moment of vertigo only existed in the crew's collective imagination.

And that, McElroy told himself as his stomach flipped again and settled nervously into its assigned space, was pure bunk. Imagination did not work collectively.

The readout screen swam before him, then focused. All green. A tiny row of symbols in the center said READY. A flick of his thumb opened the channel to *Graywand*. "Crew AA75D. Destination 3RX-99301, arrival 72.46." The chronometer above the console was now synched to *Graywand* time. During their stay on Sierra, *jack-a-dandy*'s chronometer would always be linked to *Graywand*. "No exception noted at breakout."

"Agreed," replied the commclerk, his voice still fuzzy, but no more so than when he had been only a few hundred meters away in *Graywand*'s communications center. "Co-ordination proof, please."

For the third time in the past half hour, McElroy keyed the Sierra coordinates into the control pad. The pod's brain responded immediately:

```
COORDINATES 3RX-99301
CONFIRMED ARRIVAL UNIT IDENT 1334-01-2009
AUTHORIZATION AFFIRMED PRIORITY ORANGE
HOURS—72.46 GRAYWAND CONSTANT
READY . . .
```

"Confirmed," McElroy said.

"Agreed," responded the commclerk.

A gust of wind struck *jack-a-dandy*'s port side, rocking it slightly on its pads: a reminder that the pod was no longer resting snugly inside *Graywand*'s departure dock but was instead exposed to the naked surface of Sierra. McElroy found himself trying to remember what he had read about weather conditions on Sierra. The wind felt as if it had clout behind it.

"McElroy out." He broke the connection abruptly and swung around to the others. "Everyone okay?"

"You might've warned us," Vikki snapped. She stood near the utility counter, one hand at her midsection. Her face was pale. "I feel like I'm going to be sick."

"Take a pill." McElroy's eyes moved to the others. John Wheeler sat at the far end of the counter, leafing through the Sierra background file. He looked up at McElroy and nodded almost imperceptibly. Vito Cracchiolo, taking the opportunity to move out of Vikki's line of verbal fire, stood beside Wheeler, tinkering with the jo dispenser. Stone slumped unmoving in the stationary armchair in the corner, his face the color of paste. His eyes were clenched shut.

"You okay, Tom?" McElroy asked. No response. McElroy half expected Stone to slide out of the chair and pile up on the floor like a heap of dirty laundry. "Tom?"

One hand twitched. Stone's stomach rose and fell. His

eyes opened to reddened slits. After a moment, his lips parted slightly and a single word crawled out: "Jo."

Wind struck the pod again, hard enough this time to bring creaks and groans from old joints. Something rattled against the metal skin. *Sand*, McElroy thought, frowning as something nagged at him. A breath of air from the cooling system touched his face.

They were scheduled for five days on Sierra. Not long enough for a full audit, but long enough for a close look at stores inventories and disbursement procedures. The Sierra group had been on-planet barely six months. They had spent a bundle of money getting the post established and were getting ready to spend another bundle for a new post on the other side of the planet. A good time, the Audit Agency had decided, for what they called a dollars-and-sense look at the place. McElroy and his team were there to make sure Sierra inventories were not being hauled away to help support the numerous black markets operating at UNSA expense or, more likely, being squandered away in a venture that offered little hope for a return on UNSA's investment. The United Nations Space Administration operated on a tight concept of cost/benefit relationships which required constant observation and control. The Deep Space Audit Agency covered the observation part. It was, in effect, UNSA's financial eyes and ears.

"Jo." The word came again, a painful whisper.

"Ah, poor Thomas," Cracchiolo soothed, still working with the stubborn jo dispenser. A huge grin belied the elaborately expressed sympathy. "The sauce will be the end of you. Either the sauce or the morning after. Another soul beaten by the eternal lure of the bottle."

Something continued to bother McElroy, something not quite as it should be, skirting the edges of his consciousness. He swung back to the console. All green.

His uneasy glance moved to the chronometer. They had reached the Sierra post two hours before dawn, not by choice but by the requirements of k-stream scheduling. Since the project manager would not likely be appreciative of a visiting auditor in the middle of the night, McElroy and the others were faced with three hours to kill.

The pod was rocked by another gust of wind. The wind was picking up; McElroy could hear it whispering over the pod's smooth surfaces, moaning through the web of the aft drive engine. It wasn't going to make the inventory observation any easier. Sierra was an Earthlike planet, with breathable air and tolerable climatic conditions here at the equator where the post had been established. For the most part the inventories would be stored under outside canopies; if the wind kept up, the work would be unpleasant.

"Here you are, Thomas," Cracchiolo said, behind him. "This'll fix you up."

McElroy shook his head as he reached across the console to activate the stabilizer controls. *Jack-a-dandy* lurched slightly as the extension arms moved out from their niche underneath the pod and snapped into place. McElroy's frown deepened as he felt that transitory movement, and with it a sudden discomfort, a feeling of—tension. There was no reason for it, certainly nothing in a few stout gusts of wind to cause a shiver of apprehension along his spine.

"Ah, that's good," Stone said, his voice gaining strength. He raised his cup and drank noisily as McElroy swiveled around. Stone's face had regained some of its color. He drained his cup and held it out to Cracchiolo for a refill. "And a dash of brandewine, if you please."

"That's all you need," Vikki said with an acid tone.

Stone loosed a satisfying belch. "For once I agree with you, Redford. A double dash, Crackers, if you please."

The wind outside had increased its attack against the pod, hissing and whistling through the webs of both drive engines, rising to a wail with the heavier gusts. Even with the stabilizers extended, McElroy could feel *jack-a-dandy* shift unsteadily under those blasts. The cooling unit hummed above his head.

"Sounds like we broke out in the middle of a hurricane, cap'n." Cracchiolo placed Stone's refilled cup on the ledge above the console and reached into an overhead pantry for the bottle of brandewine. "Poor *jack*'s taking a pounding."

McElroy's eyes were on John Wheeler. Wheeler had been reading through the Sierra report with his usual single-minded concentration, seemingly oblivious to everything happening around him. A moment ago his head had suddenly jerked up—the movement that caught McElroy's attention—and his eyes riveted on something near the ceiling.

The cooling unit.

That was the piece that didn't fit, the nagging something. The unit had been running steadily ever since the skip, which made no sense because Sierra was one of the coldest developed planets in *Graywand*'s realm. The post had been established at the equator for that reason, and even there the surface temperatures averaged well below freezing. McElroy and the others had brought heavy cold-weather coats for the outside inventory work. If the temperature outside was below freezing, why had *jack-a-dandy*'s cooling unit been running constantly since break-out?

McElroy turned back to the console, the shiver of apprehension hardening into something else as he flipped the row of switches that activated *jack-a-dandy*'s exterior eyes. The bank of vidscreens above the console lighted to provide a three-sixty view of the surrounding area.

McElroy sat transfixed in his chair, staring up at the screens. From the corner of his eye he saw Cracchiolo, in the act of reaching for the bottle of brandewine on the top shelf of the pantry, turn to stare, his face caught in a moment of surprise in the backwash of light from the screens.

"What the—?" began Tom Stone.

Which, McElroy thought, pretty well summed it up.

Jack-a-dandy rested on a high, rocky ledge; the bottom of the starboard screen revealed the jutting edge dropping off far below. But McElroy's attention was drawn to the more distant view: sunlight glaring down over a harsh valley, a ribbed gully snaking through a scratchy landscape, low scrub hugging brown-baked sand. Farther back, smudged with distance, lay a rugged mountain range crowded on one side by dense forest. In conspicuous absence were the buildings, surface pads, and metalfilm canopies of a UNSA post. McElroy felt the wind touch the pod. He shivered.

"Hey, cap'n," Crackers asked quietly. "Where the heck *are* we?"

CHAPTER TWO

Cracchiolo's question went unanswered. A brittle silence settled over them, interrupted only by the moan of the wind and the rattle of sand and the sounds of *jack-a-dandy* going about its business: the buzz-blip of the readout screen, the faint click of control relays, the hushed tones of the sounder.

"This is not Sierra," McElroy murmured, unable to take his eyes away from the screens.

After a long moment Vikki Redford said simply, "It *has* to be Sierra."

She was right. The barren world that stretched so vividly across *jack-a-dandy*'s vidscreen had to be Sierra because *Graywand*'s navigation computer had sent them to Sierra. It was the nature of k-stream skips that you either arrived on target or you did not arrive at all. There was no almost-making-it, no chance of missing target by a hundred meters or a kilometer or a light-year. An error during breakout could not result in anything less than disaster. Rare as such errors were, they were always fatal.

All this went through McElroy's mind as he looked out on that bleak panorama and felt the pod shudder under another strong gust of wind.

"Someone goofed," said Cracchiolo. "Think we can ungoof it, cap'n?"

Yes, McElroy told himself, *someone has surely goofed.* He reached for the commbox.

"*Graywand*. This is McElroy, AA75D. Acknowledge, please."

After a moment: "*Graywand* here, AA75D."

McElroy glanced again at the vidscreens, wondering if it were possible that they were all the victims of some sort of bizarre joke. Outside, the sand was kicking up in swirling funnels, rattling against the pod with increased force. "There is no sign of the Sierra post," he said at last. "There's no sign of development of any kind."

The reply to this was a moment coming. "The Sierra post is deserted?"

"Negative," McElroy corrected tersely. "There *is* no post. We've skipped to the wrong place. Vegetation and topography do not match Sierra background reports."

Another pause, longer this time. "You're saying break-out did not take place at Sierra? I don't—"

"Is this Clemens?"

"Yes, sir—"

McElroy drew a breath. "Listen to me, Mr. Clemens. Something went wrong with the skip. I don't know what or how, and to tell you the truth, I am not inclined to have a theoretical discussion of the matter right now. What I am interested in is getting back to *Graywand*."

Silence from the commbox. McElroy could almost feel the commclerk chewing through what he had been told. "Sir, the Sierra post was established on 31.23, *Graywand* constant—"

"Let me speak to your supervisor."

"I'm sorry, sir, there's no one available at the moment."

"Mr. Clemens, I am requesting immediate return to *Graywand*. I want it now, right now."

Another long silence came from the commbox. McElroy unclenched his fists, easing the tension that had knotted in his neck and shoulders. "Clemens?"

"Right here, sir. I'm working through the computations." The young commclerk's voice had steadied, as if he too had taken a moment to collect himself. "The stream schedule is set, Mr. McElroy. I may be able to destabilize it and pull an opening in three hours. Until then I can't bypass it without endangering others already in the cycle."

"Get Spalding." Robert Spalding was head of CommSec operations services. An incompetent ass in McElroy's opinion, but at least he had authority to render a decision in a matter like this.

"He isn't available, sir."

"Listen, Clemens—"

"He's right, cap'n." Cracchiolo's voice, and the hand on his shoulder, defused McElroy's explosion before it could reach critical term. "About the schedule, I mean."

McElroy spun around to Cracchiolo. "Are you sure about that?"

Cracchiolo nodded. "A few years ago I took some training in stream mechanics. The kid knows what he's talking about. If they try to interrupt a cycle that's already set, they run the risk of getting the navigation brain mixed up. Might get its signals crossed and flip someone into never-never land. Like us, for example."

"It would appear," Wheeler observed quietly, "that it already has."

Cracchiolo grinned. "Wrong, brother John. This is somewhere. Never-never land is *nowhere*."

McElroy looked at Cracchiolo for a moment, then turned back to the commbox. "You there, Clemens?"

"Right here, sir."

"Can you hear that roaring sound from your end?"

"I can hear it, sir."

"That isn't background static. That's the wind. Sixty

knots, I'd guess. Not exactly a gentle breeze. If we don't get out of here soon, it's going to pound this old junkbucket to pieces."

"I understand, sir."

"Three hours?"

After a brief hesitation: "Perhaps earlier, sir, if I can juggle the schedule. I'll do what I can."

"Thank you, Mr. Clemens. We'll be waiting. McElroy out." He broke the connection, leaned back in the chair, and let his gaze drift to the unchanging view on the vidscreens.

The brief silence was broken by Vikki, who asked the question that was on all their minds. "Can the pod take three hours of this?"

"Sure," said Stone, but there was more hope than confidence in his voice. "Little buggers are made for this kind of treatment."

McElroy could see more details now, some of the reasons for the inhospitable look of the place. The valley below, filling the fore screen, had a starkly barren look to it. Only a few clumps of reddish-brown vegetation and a half-dozen scraggly growths that might be called trees broke through the parched ground. The vegetation was low and sturdy, clumped for the most part around rocky knolls. The smudge of forest was too far away to see in detail, but even from a distance it had a sinister look to it. Not the sort of place for an afternoon stroll. The view on the aft screen was even less inviting: a mass of solid rock rising nakedly under the glaring sun. All of it was treacherous territory. McElroy turned to look at the others. "Anyone got any ideas?"

"Just one, cap'n." Cracchiolo closed the pantry door and held up the nearly full bottle of brandewine. "Let's get snizzed."

"Splendid idea," Stone said in immediate and predictable agreement. He had not moved from his slumped position in the corner chair. He looked better, though, than when he had come aboard the pod. "You manage to come up with a decent one now and then."

Cracchiolo chuckled good-naturedly, but the light comments did not fit the situation, and they all knew it. A routine skip had turned into a jumble of confusion; somehow *Graywand*'s navigation computer had slipped and sent them to an uninhabited region of—somewhere. They felt the strangeness pressing at them, felt it there outside the pod in the swirling sand and the desolate landscape on the vidscreens. They did not belong here; everything they saw and heard told them so. Was the atmosphere breathable? Would *jack-a-dandy* be able to withstand that battering wind? Was there dangerous animal life? Or, God forbid, were there intelligents that might drop by for a visit? Those questions and others were beginning to register. McElroy could see it in the faces of the others, in the way their eyes flicked nervously from one to another and to the vidscreens.

He turned abruptly to Cracchiolo and grumbled, "What's the holdup? Start pouring."

"Sure, cap'n." Cracchiolo turned to the cabinet beside the pantry and reached for the plastiform cups, and with that single act of reaching provided the final nudge that sent them over the brink into the nightmare.

Cracchiolo was a small man, thin and wiry, with scarcely enough meat on his bones to hold them together. But slight as it was, his weight, when he stepped into the corner of the pod and reached into the cabinet, was enough to push an already weakened stabilizer gear past its breaking point.*
The brace gave way with an emphatic thump and the stabilizer collapsed, bringing one corner of *jack-a-dandy*

---

*Later, when each detail of the Tartarus incident was subjected to the closest scrutiny, one of the investigating teams found buried in *jack-a-dandy*'s service file a technician's observation that the joint of an elbow brace inside that particular stabilizer appeared to be weakened. Why the technician had chosen to write up that minor item rather than simply replace the elbow brace himself was a matter discussed at some length during the subsequent hearings.

crashing down on the rock ledge with enough force to send Cracchiolo sprawling. The bottle of brandewine smashed on the graymetal floor amid a cacophony of creaks and pops as the pod twisted and settled its weight on the remaining three stabilizers.

After a moment they began breathing again. Cracchiolo broke the silence as he got to his feet, his clothing soaked with brandewine. "Sorry, cap'n. Guess we can't get snizzed."

"Crackers, you clumsy oaf," Stone said with a resigned tone. "Should've known you would lose our only bottle—"

"*What happened*?" Vikki exploded. "What's going on—?"

"Calm down," McElroy ordered harshly. "We're getting out of here. One way or another, they can break that schedule." He turned back to the console, bracing himself against the crazy tilt of the floor. The wind rose to a crescendo, shrieking against the side of the pod. The console was a mess; the cup Cracchiolo had set on the ledge had fallen, spilling jo across the control pad. A stream of it soaked McElroy's pantleg as he moved in under the console. Ignoring it, he reached across to the commbox, ready to spill out a firm demand for an immediate return to *Graywand*. At any minute the wind could snatch *jack-a-dandy* from its precarious perch and send it crashing to the rocks below. He wanted them away from this place.

"*Graywand*. This is McElroy, AA75D."

The usual prompt response from the *Graywand* commclerk did not come. Even before the absence of response sank in, McElroy knew something was wrong. The commbox was dead. No background static, no hollow feedback. Nothing. He pressed the switch again and again, with the same result.

A question was asked behind him, but McElroy kept silent, his eyes moving across the console. Then he saw the brown puddle—the spilled jo—at the base of the commbox unit, trickling down behind it.

"It isn't possible, cap'n." Cracchiolo had seen it, too. He moved closer to look over McElroy's shoulder, his boots crunching in the broken glass. "Even these old pods have all kinds of backup circuits. No way a little spilled jo could short it out."

"Then, what's wrong?"

Cracchiolo shook his head. "I got no idea, cap'n. Never heard of a commbox going out before. Don't see how it could, to tell you the truth."

Vikki Redford looked first at Cracchiolo, then at McElroy. "You aren't saying we're stranded in this godforsaken place," she said tentatively. "Are you?"

"We aren't stranded," McElroy told her. "There's nothing to worry about." *Then why is your own stomach tying itself into knots?* "Someone will be along after us any minute."

"If they can." John Wheeler had not moved from his place at the counter through everything that had happened. The Sierra file still lay open before him. He was a slight man, thin almost to the point of emaciation. The strained look on his face was a permanent part of him. He shrugged now as everyone turned to look at him. "They may not be able to find us."

"What are you talking about?" McElroy demanded. "They sent us here. Why shouldn't they be able to come after us?"

Wheeler's bony shoulders moved again in a faint shrug, his pale eyes on the bank of vidscreens above McElroy's head. One blue-veined hand moved to the heavy bronze amulet that always hung around his neck. "If we aren't on Sierra, where are we?"

"How am I supposed to know? The idiots on *Graywand* sent us here."

"Not exactly. The *Graywand* navigator sent us here. A computer, not a person. As far as the commclerk was concerned, we were going to Sierra."

McElroy started to say something, then closed his mouth as the realization hit him.

"You see my point?" Wheeler formed a thin smile. His eyes were still on the vidscreens, as if held there by a spell. "If they don't know where we are, how can they come after us?"

CHAPTER THREE

In *Graywand*'s Communications Services Section, usually referred to as CommSec, Lars Clemens was quietly going berserk.

Lars was one of twelve commclerks stationed in a crowded CommSec operations room on *Graywand*'s second level, just aft of the operations executive offices. The commclerks were *Graywand*'s first-level liaison with its support vehicles. Communications with other sector ships were the domain of CommSec officers higher up the scale; communications with UNSA regional bases, rare as they were through complex stream connections, were limited to the top cadre of *Graywand* executive officers.

Each commclerk had his own cubicle, complete with commbox, control pad, readout screen, and a red handset that provided intercom connection to the executive officer, for use in an emergency.

Lars's eyes kept straying to the red handset. For the first time in the few short months he had been on *Gray-*

wand, he found himself wondering what constituted an emergency.

Ten minutes earlier he'd freed an opening in the stream cycle, a spot barely an hour away, that gave room for a return of McElroy and his team. Then he'd found he could not make contact with McElroy. He had stared dumbfounded at his commbox for a moment, then moved to Carl Lunsford's unit in an adjacent cubicle. Once again he keyed in the Sierra coordinate variation that should have linked him to McElroy's pod. Still nothing.

Which was impossible. Which meant, he told himself, that he had an emergency. He reached for the red handset.

"Better not," warned Lunsford, "unless you're sure you have something big."

Lars snatched his hand away as if the handset had burned him. "I can't just sit here. I have to do something."

Lunsford's mind was on a regression riddle that was spread out across his control pad. He was not especially interested in Clemens's problem, but he saw it as his duty to keep the kid out of trouble—as long as he could do so and still avoid buying any trouble of his own. "It's your neck. Personally, I think your audit-types will show up. You and McElroy must've gotten your confirmations screwed up. They've skipped to some other post, that's all."

"There's only one post on Sierra," Lars pointed out.

Lunsford shrugged. He leaned back and propped his feet up on the console shelf, his brow furrowing as he studied the series of lines and symbols he'd marked across the face of the riddle. "All I'm saying is, you'd better clear it with Spalding before you hit the panic button."

"I can't *find* Spalding."

Lunsford jotted a note on the riddle, then grinned with satisfaction as a pattern fell into place. "Did you try the Cornucopia?"

"The Cornucopia?" Lars glanced at the chronometer. It was still early morning by *Graywand* reckoning.

"He knows Kabrinski, the manager," Lunsford explained.

"Goes in sometimes to shoot the breeze and have spiced jo. That's the story, anyway."

Lars was mildly surprised when his call to the Cornucopia was answered. He was even more surprised, and intensely relieved, when he was put through to Robert Spalding.

Spalding heard him out, then asked, "Oliver McElroy, you say?"

"Yes, sir. And four others. McElroy is a field senior with the Audit Agency."

"He claims they broke out in the wrong place?"

"That's right, sir."

Spalding thought for a moment. "Maybe you'd better call him back and recheck that. It all sounds pretty unlikely to me."

Somehow Spalding had missed the major point of what Lars had told him. "I can't, sir. The commbox isn't operating."

"Use someone else's," Spalding suggested.

"Not *my* commbox, sir. McElroy's." Lars felt beads of sweat breaking out on his forehead. "I can't get through to him because *his* commbox is malfunctioning."

"Maybe you're using the wrong coordinates." Spalding seemed to be having trouble absorbing what Lars told him.

"I checked that, sir. First thing. I used the same coordinates that were used for the skip."

"That's the problem, then. The wrong coordinates were used for the skip." Spalding's voice had taken on the self-satisfied tone of someone who has solved a long and complex problem. "They probably broke out at some other post. We'll be hearing from them before long."

"If that were so, I still should be able to get through to them. Even if the wrong coordinates were used for the skip, those same coordinates should put us through to them. Besides, I've verified the Sierra coordinates with the navigation computer."

Spalding breathed into Lars's headset while he digested

this new information. "Maybe they haven't responded to the call because they're out of the pod."

"It isn't like that, sir. The signal won't track. It isn't a matter of nobody acknowledging—"

"Call the Sierra post, then." Spalding's voice took on an edge of impatience as he began to run out of suggestions. "Find out if they've seen anything."

"I already have. They've had no breakouts since yesterday. They're looking around, but—"

"Something must've gotten fouled up in the schedule. You confirmed with McElroy before the skip?"

"Yes, sir." How long, Lars wondered, could this last?

"Well, you and McElroy must've gotten your wires crossed. Use your scanning scope to backtrack through the coordination check. Run a simulation to check it out if you have to. I'll be down in a few minutes." The channel went dead.

"Thank you, sir," Lars muttered belatedly. He clicked off and stared woodenly at the glowing cluster of lights at the top of his control board.

"Not much help, huh?"

Lars's head jerked around to Lunsford. "What?"

"Spalding. I assume he handed you the usual high-level lack of support. Nuts." The "nuts" was for the regression riddle: Lunsford was having trouble finding the pattern in the final series. He jotted down another pair of symbols, then grimaced and scribbled them out.

"He wants me to backtrack with the scanner," Lars said numbly. "He said to run a simulation model through the navigator."

Lunsford issued a short bark of laughter. "Old Spalding's a little out of touch." Backtracking and simulation models were diagnostics used by the CommSec techs to test for component weakness in the control boards. Neither could be of even remote benefit to the problem at hand. "You'd better get this straightened out before he gets down here. He'll only make it worse."

"How can *I* straighten it out?" Nobody seemed to grasp

the fact that they faced a serious problem. "There was a technical error in the skip. I talked to McElroy afterwards. They broke out in the wrong place. It's as simple as that."

"And a technical problem with the commbox, too? It gets a bit hard to follow at that point. Sounds more like a coordination problem to me."

Lars shook his head but kept silent. There could not have been an error in the coordinates. He had gone through it a dozen times in his mind: the confirmations between McElroy and himself; coordinates verified before and after the skip; internal verifications with *Graywand*'s navigation computer. There was no way the coordinates could have been wrong. Nor was there any chance he and McElroy could have misunderstood the schedule. McElroy and his crew had been bound for Sierra, but they never arrived. And then McElroy's commbox malfunctioned.

One impossibility after another. A stack of them, building up to place five people in limbo with no way back to *Graywand*. And Robert Spalding's solution was to run a simulation model.

"Heads up," Lunsford said. "You have a signal."

The light on the commbox pulsed green. Lars acknowledged the call and was rewarded by a rasping voice that rattled through his headset.

"Clawson here." Rod Clawson was project manager on Sierra. "They aren't here. We looked all over."

Lars glanced at the chronometer. It had been forty minutes since he'd contacted Clawson, an interval of time short enough to cause doubt in his mind about the adequacy of Clawson's search.

"Only one place a pod can break out on our little snowball," Clawson went on. "Take my word for it, they aren't here. Went out and sniffed around for myself, and I'll tell you, kid, I can smell an auditor a mile away." Clawson spoke with the tone of the overworked operations manager long accustomed to dealing with the idiocies of *Graywand* command. "Think it might be okay if I get back to bed now?"

"Mr. Clawson, can you think of anything that might explain what happened? I've lost contact with them and—"

"That's what happens when you screw up the coordinates."

I did not screw up the coordinates!

"They didn't make it to Sierra, kid. That's all I know. Which means the coordinates were wrong, because there just isn't any other way for a skip to go haywire. But don't feel so bad about it. It happens now and then. A few weeks ago a Blue popped in here by mistake for the same reason. Just didn't take care with the coordinates. Don't get all heated up about your audit boys. They'll turn up."

Lars muttered a terse thanks and broke the connection. He leaned back in his chair and went back through it yet again. His confirmations with McElroy, verification by the navigation computer, all tests greened through. There was nothing out of place; everything was routine right up to the skip. *"That's the wind. Sixty knots, I'd guess. If we don't get out of here, it's going to pound this old junkbucket to pieces."*

"Uh-oh," murmured Carl Lunsford.

Lars turned in his chair as Robert Spalding stepped through the sliding doors of the elevator and headed purposefully in their direction.

CHAPTER FOUR

"Ouch! Stop crowding me, Crackers."

Tom Stone jerked his hand out of the disassembled
mess that had been the commbox switch and looked at
the scrape that was already beginning to ooze blood along
his index finger. He was not comfortable in his awkward
position under the console, trying to work on the switch
mechanism and brace himself against the pitch of the
floor at the same time. He did not have the tools or
experience for the job and had volunteered to help
Cracchiolo—who supposedly *did* know what he was
doing—only because anything was better than sitting
around waiting for something to happen. Even with the
cooling unit laboring at full speed, he was sticky with
sweat. The *sake* hangover still thumped uneasily inside
his head, and his usual good nature had been pushed beyond
reasonable limits. Vito Cracchiolo, working above him on
the commbox circuitry, was the closest target for his
frustrations.

The injury to Stone's finger, which was the result of his own carelessness with a screwdriver, proved to be less than serious. A quick dab with his handkerchief quelled the trickle of blood.

"Sorry, Thomas." Cracchiolo stepped back onto Vikki's foot. "Uh-oh."

"Watch what you're doing," Vikki snapped.

"Sorry." Cracchiolo turned back to Stone. "Let me in there, Thomas. I'm all done up here. Besides, my hands are little bitty things, special made for—"

"Never mind," Stone interrupted irritably. "I've almost got it."

Although there was little humor in their situation, Oliver McElroy, watching from the corner chair, had to smile. *Jack-a-dandy* was barely larger than an oversize shoebox, and had not been designed to hold five people in comfort.

"Ouch!" Stone exclaimed as the screwdriver slipped again and bit into the flesh of his finger. "This is insanity! I'm an accountant, not a mechanic."

McElroy offered no comment. His fingers tapped a three-count rhythm on the arm of the chair; his eyes moved repeatedly to the vidscreen above the console, and he kept thinking about the question Wheeler had asked. *What if they don't know where we are?*

"Got it," Stone muttered at last. He crawled backwards out of the shallow workspace, the commbox switch held tightly in one large fist. He looked at it for a moment, then handed it across to Cracchiolo. "Now what?"

Cracchiolo probed at welded seams and tugged cautiously at wires. His mouth formed a small frown. "There's nothing loose, no burned-out terminals or anything like that." He looked up at McElroy and gave an apologetic shrug. "Whatever's wrong with it, there's no way we're going to fix it, cap'n. It's a sealed unit."

"We've *got* to fix it." Vikki Redford stood beside Cracchiolo, looking down at the switch mechanism. "Take it apart if you have to."

"Simmer down," McElroy interrupted. "We can't take

it apart. That's what Crackers means. Not with the tools we have.''

Vikki turned to face McElroy. "That's great. We can't fix the commbox, we can't contact *Graywand*, we can't get out of this place. So what're we going to do?"

The problem, they had decided, had to be in the switch—the mechanism under the console that accepted stored power from the drive system and transformed it into energy the commbox could use. The switch was the only electronic component of the communications system. Most likely, they'd decided, it had been damaged by the spilled jo.

"Can you bypass it?" McElroy asked Cracchiolo.

"Bypass it?" Cracchiolo looked doubtful.

"Connect the commbox directly to the spud."

Cracchiolo's brow wrinkled as he thought it over. "Might work, cap'n. Depends on how much juice the box can take."

"What's our risk?"

Cracchiolo thought for a moment longer. "Tops would be a frizzled commbox."

"Then let's try it. The commbox isn't doing us much good anyway."

"You got it, cap'n." Cracchiolo kicked away a shard of glass that had been missed during cleanup and lowered himself to the floor. He squirmed agilely into the workspace and began stripping insulation from wires.

McElroy returned to the corner chair, leaned back against the hard cushion, and raised his eyes again to the row of vidscreens. The fore screen was flickering. They'd had problems with it before—something that seemed to defy permanent repair by *Graywand*'s mechanics. The erratic flickering would, he knew, worsen and the screen would blank out for good—or at least until the mechanics had another go at it.

Not that he would mind if it did go out. The valley below—the stunted trees and the reddish-brown vegetation and that rock-strewn gully snaking out across it—did not present a comforting landscape. He shifted his eyes to the chronometer. Barely two hours had passed since they had lost contact with *Graywand*.

How can they come after us if they don't know where we are?

Damn Wheeler, anyway, and his clinical observations. But even as he cursed Wheeler a small voice inside him said: *If they were coming, they would have been here by now*.

Vikki Redford made a sound—a long, jittery exhalation of breath. She sat on one of the backless stools, leaning against the counter in what looked to be an uncomfortable position, staring up at the vidscreens. Beside her John Wheeler, still wearing a thin smile, also watched the screens. Tom Stone, sitting on the floor awaiting instructions from Cracchiolo, seemed to be too tired to do anything but close his eyes and produce more sweat.

Why are we so fragile? McElroy thought.

Their lives, so neatly wrapped in patterned experience, had been stripped clean of meaningful definition. They knew nothing of what lay in the barren valley, or beyond in the dark forest. The shields of constancy were down. They faced the unknown—that ancient horror of human-kind. There were no familiar patterns in their new envi-ronment, no learned ways of dealing with this feeling of helplessness they had never before faced.

"Looks like a ninety-nine."

Wheeler's quiet statement sliced like a blade through McElroy's thoughts. His eyes jerked across to the older man. "A ninety-nine?"

Wheeler gestured toward the vidscreen. "Lots of vege-tation. Air may be breathable." A ninety-nine was the informal designation for a planet with Earthlike characteris-tics sufficient to support human life. The ninety-nine in the Sierra coordinates—3RX-99301—identified it as such a planet. This planet, as Wheeler pointed out, had every appearance of also being a ninety-nine, although a week or more of study by the Blue's research teams would be required before it could be given official recognition as such.

"You planning on taking a walk, John?" Vikki asked.

Wheeler smiled faintly. "Just thought I'd mention it. In case we're stranded here for good."

He's done it again, McElroy said to himself

Vikki swung around, mouth gaping. "Damn you, Wheeler. You always act like you think you're something special—"

McElroy held up a restraining hand. "That's enough."

"Well, I've had it with—"

"Vikki!" McElroy fixed her with a hard look. "Quiet down."

Vikki clenched her teeth with a snap and turned away, fuming.

"We can try it now, cap'n." Cracchiolo climbed out of the workspace and rose to his feet. "Only thing is—" He glanced tentatively at Tom Stone. "Well, I'll need somebody to support the switch housing under the shelf while I connect it up."

Stone roused himself and looked across at Cracchiolo. With a resigned sigh, he slid across the floor and eased himself once again into the space under the console. Cracchiolo knelt down to give him brief instructions. "Okay, cap'n," he said, gesturing to McElroy. "If it works, we won't have much time."

"Coming." McElroy stepped over Stone's outstretched legs to the console. Maybe they would get lucky. They were due some luck. "Ready?"

Cracchiolo reached into the tangle of wires and made a series of connections. Holding it all in place, he nodded assent.

McElroy hesitated only a moment, then pressed the commbox switch.

Something crackled underneath the console. Stone roared and slammed his head against the underside of the shelf, then skittered out backwards, flapping his hand wildly. A trail of smoke spiraled upwards from the commbox, carrying an odor of scorched insulation.

"Uh-oh," said Cracchiolo. He released his hold on the wiring harnesses and helped Stone to his feet. "Thomas, are you hurt?"

McElroy stared at the tiny wisp of smoke, too concerned with what it meant to be solicitous of Stone. With that crackle of electricity and wisp of smoke had gone their last chance to contact *Graywand*. Which meant they were down to one option.

"Work them out manually?" Vikki asked incredulously. "Is it possible?"

"Sure," McElroy said, hoping he was right. "And you've just volunteered to help do it."

"Me?" Vikki's eyes widened. "I don't know the first thing about stream coordinates."

"You have a logical mind. That's all you need. I've been through it before. It's a piece of cake. Besides, if you ever expect to get into Field Recon, you'll need the experience."

"Listen, McElroy—"

But McElroy had already turned to the console to begin querying *jack-a-dandy* for preliminary information. Vikki stared at him for a moment, then her eyes rolled heavenward as if seeking mercy, and a long, weary sigh emerged from somewhere deep inside her. "All right. What do you want me to do?"

"Hang loose for a minute." McElroy concentrated on what was becoming a frustrating conversation with *jack-a-dandy*. What he had said about having been through this before was only partly true: during his two years at the Kominsk Academy on Terra, while nurturing thoughts of a career in Field Recon, he had taken general training in emergency procedures which included skipping blind. For Field Recon crews, skipping without the benefit of sector ship navigation support was a rare, but not unheard of, occurrence. Bounding as they did through the vague substance of the stream in search of new planets, Field Recon pods sometimes inadvertently broke free of sector ship control, popping out in uncharted territory with no way to contact NavSec for aid in returning. When McElroy assured Vikki of his experience with blind skips, he saw no reason to mention that such experience had been entirely academic.

"Find some paper," he told her as he jabbed a command into the console. "And something to write with. The rest of you stay out of our hair."

A few minutes later they were deep into it.

It was tiring work, and it took a lot longer than McElroy had expected. *Jack-a-dandy*'s brain was an operational tool that was not programmed for the kind of analysis needed to compute *Graywand*'s coordinates. It knew where to find *Graywand* by looking back through the skip sequence it had made, but it could not tell its human companions in a way they could easily grasp. Nor could it make the skip on its own without a locking signal from *Graywand*'s navigation computer. Drawing from *jack-a-dandy* the information necessary to provide a false locking signal was a back-and-forth process that called for mental concentration and exhausting checks and rechecks. McElroy knew that if one step were misplaced, the entire sequence would break down; they could never be absolutely certain of their answers until McElroy pressed the blue button to activate the pod's drive engines. If a single equation were wrong, they would find themselves spread across Omega, stripped atom from atom by the opposing stresses.

They'd been at it for three hours, by which time they had thoroughly skinned and boiled one another's nerves, when they moved to the counter and spread their workpapers out for a final check.

They ran through their tests for the last time, glared at one another for a long moment, then agreed that they were finished. The coordinates were ready.

"Thank God," Vikki muttered.

McElroy sipped cold jo and tapped keys on the control

pad, all his concentration focused on the worksheets spread out in front of him and the green figures trailing across the readout screen. He ran a coherence test at each step, using a stubby pencil to place a checkmark beside each equation on the worksheet as it passed muster.

The final equation pulsed across the screen at last and was followed by: READY. McElroy placed the pencil on the console with exaggerated care, leaned back in the control chair, and covered his eyes with both palms.

It should work, he told himself. *The pieces fit together as they should. They seem to, anyway. No reason at all why it shouldn't work—*

Someone touched his arm. "You okay, cap'n?"

He took his hands away and looked up at Cracchiolo. Then he grinned wearily. "No arguments, Crackers. I'm buying the first round at the Cornucopia."

"Ho! Won't find an argument in me, cap'n."

"Me neither," chimed in Stone, his old congeniality back. He raised his cup of jo in a toast, then downed it in one gulp and brought forth a magnificent belch. "I'll buy the second, and Redford can buy the third."

"Let's just get on with it," Vikki grumped from her place at the counter.

McElroy turned back to the console, drew a breath, and began talking *jack-a-dandy* through the final preparations for the skip. Despite his exhaustion, he worked briskly, eager to get it over with. He felt good about their chances now. The equations were solid. Everything had been checked and rechecked. Ten minutes from now they would be inside *Graywand*'s hold. And despite what he had said about the Cornucopia, his first visit would be to the Navigation Section, where he had every intention of batting heads around until a few answers popped out.

Reaching automatically to the rear panel of the console, he depressed a row of switches to shut down auxiliary power, retract stabilizer gears, activate autocontrol systems—

The stabilizer control glowed amber. Malfunction.

McElroy stared at the blinking light, not wanting to believe it. He made a sound deep in his throat.

Vikki Redford's head jerked up. "What's wrong?"

"Amber hold," McElroy answered in a flat tone.

"I can see that—"

"Stabilizer's jammed. Must be the one that was damaged earlier. It won't retract."

"So what's the big deal? Let it hang there."

A long moment of silence was broken by Cracchiolo. "We can't. The stream won't take us with the stabilizers out."

"Why not?" Vikki demanded. "Can't we override it?"

Cracchiolo shook his head, smiling apologetically. "*Jack*'s gotta give a smooth surface. Can't have lumpy things like stabilizers hanging out when he skips."

"Well that's wonderful. What are we supposed to do?"

Cracchiolo had no answer for that. Apparently nobody did. McElroy worked the stabilizer switch back and forth several times while the amber light blinked steadily. "Here's what we do," he said at last, pronouncing each word with care. "We go outside, crawl under the pod, and take a hammer to the stabilizer."

"The problem with that," John Wheeler pointed out, "is that we don't know what the air is like out there. It may not be breathable."

"Yes," McElroy agreed dryly, "that could be a problem."

"We don't have to do it," Vikki Redford argued. "We can sit here and wait. Help will be coming before long."

McElroy shook his head in disagreement. "That's exactly what we can't do. We don't know if help will be coming or not, and we can't wait any longer to find out. The wind could kick up again any time. If it blows even a little harder than before, we'll be in trouble. I'm not prepared to take the risk of getting us blown off this ledge."

"Uh, cap'n?" Cracchiolo was looking through the supply bin at the far end of the pod. He had a puzzled look on his face. "We've got a—"

"That's fine, McElroy," Vikki snapped, her eyes flaring. "But what about the risk of breathing poisonous air if we open that hatchcover?" She faced him squarely, hands planted on her hips. "All I'm saying is, we should hold off opening the hatch as long as possible."

"And I'm saying we already have."

Stone cleared his throat. "The thing is, we won't be taking that much of a risk by opening it up." Vikki shot him a withering look that he withstood with a slight hunching of his bearlike shouders. "The air should be all right. It can't be too bad, not with all the trees and plantlife out there."

"That doesn't mean we can breathe it," Vikki cut in harshly.

"Listen, folks," Cracchiolo tried again from the aft section of the pod. "There's something here we should—"

"Screen's out."

McElroy's eyes jerked sideways to John Wheeler's unperturbed face, then moved to the bank of vidscreens. The fore screen was dark, shot through with streamers of light.

That, McElroy told himself angrily, was the final straw. Never again would he accept this old broken-down excuse for a pod. Never.

Just below the vidscreens, on the graymetal surface above the rear panel of the console, was a long row of faded black letters: GENERAL SERVICES AUDIT AGENCY—DEEP SPACE GROUP. The line was not centered properly under the screen; whoever had changed the inscription from FIELD RECONNAISSANCE—DEEP SPACE GROUP when the pod was transferred to the Audit Agency had apparently been more concerned with efficiency than with making the inscription a work of art, and so had merely obliterated the words FIELD RECON-NAISSANCE and replaced them with the longer title identifying the General Services Audit Agency. The line was skewed to the left, and the word SPACE lay directly beneath the fore screen. While the inscription was not particularly aesthetic, it nonetheless did offer a convenient target for McElroy's wrath. He raised a fist and struck the word SPACE, giving it all the frustrations of the past six hours in one mighty blow. The vidscreen blinked twice and came to life.

The barren valley, the slashing gully, the distant forest—all were exactly as before. A gust of wind tugged at the pod. McElroy rubbed his stinging knuckles and felt immensely better.

"Okay," he said, pushing himself out of the control chair. "Let's see what tools we can find."

"Already have, cap'n." Cracchiolo grinned across at them, holding an enormous spanner in one hand and a pry bar in the other.

"You found those in the supply hold?" McElroy asked incredulously.

"Sure. All kinds of other goodies, too. Bet it's been there since *jack* was with Field Recon." Cracchiolo hefted the spanner. "Biggest sonofagun I ever saw." He hesitated. "One other thing I noticed in the supply hold, cap'n. Been trying to tell you, but you were all too busy to listen."

"Yeah?"

Cracchiolo's smile had turned into something that looked suspiciously like a sly grin. "Well . . . you noticed, I guess, that it's been getting kinda warm in here."

McElroy had noticed. Even with the cooling unit running steadily, the temperature inside the pod had been climbing. Their faces gleamed with sweat. "What about it?"

Cracchiolo's grin broadened. "If you guys had let me get a word in edgeways, I'd have told you that you were arguing a dead issue. Old *jack*'s split a seam. Probably happened when the stabilizer gave way. There's a hole as big as my Aunt Annie's fanny in the back wall of the hold."

McElroy's brow wrinkled. He felt a little scrambled. "It goes through to the outside?"

"Yep. You could reach right through it and touch the ground if you wanted to."

"Then that means . . ." Vikki's voice trailed off.

"It means," McElroy finished for her, "that we've been breathing this planet's atmosphere for some time." Wheeler was right. It was a ninety-nine.

When all was said and done, Tom Stone was selected to go out and fix the jammed stabilizer gear. McElroy was adamant that only one person leave the pod. Flabby and out of shape as he was, Stone was nonetheless a powerful man; if freeing the gear depended on brute strength, Stone had the best chance of any of them.

As it turned out, the job was ludicrously easy. With one solid swing of the monstrous spanner, Stone straightened a brace that had buckled inward and jammed against the gear housing. A moment later he clambered back through the hatchway and collapsed panting and gasping into the corner chair. "It must be a hundred twenty degrees out there."

An understatement, McElroy guessed. Even in the few moments the hatchcover had been raised, the temperature inside *jack-a-dandy* had risen considerably. The air was hot and dry, with a tangy odor that was just short of being unpleasant.

Not that it matters, he told himself. Graywand *will be cool and comfortable.*

The others crowded around as he settled into the control chair, his eyes on the amber pulse of the stabilizer control. A lot rested on that tiny piece of plastic. He reached out and depressed it, silently commanding compliance from the stabilizer gear. Movement came from under the pod, resolving into a steady downward motion. The floor tilted crazily, then leveled. The pads at the base of each stabilizer crunched into solid rock. The amber light winked to green.

"All right!" yelled Cracchiolo. He clapped McElroy on the back. "We did it, cap'n."

"Cornucopia, here we come," said Stone. "Order me a hot *sake*, McElroy."

"Somebody's going to pay for this," Vikki muttered.

McElroy vowed silent agreement as he scanned the row of green lights at the back of the console. The readout screen said DRIVE SYSTEM READY. *It's going to be okay*, he thought wonderingly. *After everything that's happened, it's going to work out after all.*

He lifted the safety cover, braced himself for the punch, and thumbed the blue lever.

Nothing happened. No drunk-stagger. No punch in the gut. Nothing.

A gust of wind rattled sand against the pod, and moved on.

CHAPTER FIVE

"You confirmed the coordinates prior to the skip?"

"Yes, sir."

"McElroy agreed with the authorized destination?"

"Completely, sir. There was no reason to—"

"NavSec affirmed said authorization?"

Said authorization? "Through standard navigation procedures, sir." Raymond Spick, *Graywand* CommSec Director, had a way of looking at you that made you want to squirm. Lars resisted by an effort of will. "I've checked the log, sir. Everything was covered."

"Apparently not everything," Spick responded dryly. "Something most assuredly went wrong. We would not be having this discussion if something had not gone wrong."

The third man in the room cleared his throat. "I asked Lars to pull a hard copy of his conversation with McElroy." Robert Spalding leaned across the desk to hand the yellow transcript to Spick. Spalding was as nervous as Lars, a fact which did not make the young commclerk feel better. And

Spalding had just told a blatant lie: Lars had taken it entirely upon himself to pull the transcript. "Looks to me as if they pretty well covered it." Then, hastily: "Although I haven't had time to look at it closely. I thought we should get to you right away."

Another barefaced lie. Spalding had wasted the better part of an hour going over the details of Lars's dialogue with Oliver McElroy. Lars had sweated through the grilling, thinking of McElroy and the others stranded and out of touch with *Graywand* while Spalding doggedly traced through the transcript, asking questions that were meant to display sharp incisiveness but which only revealed his own ignorance of CommSec procedures.

Raymond Spick scanned the transcript, his beetle brows knitted, making small sounds of grudging concurrence as he read. Suddenly he stopped, his features screwing together in an overplayed grimace. Spick was a small man, slightly hunched, with a large head that had only a fringe of graying hair at the temples. He was given to exaggerated facial expressions because of a mistaken belief that such expressions distracted from his dwarfish appearance. Instead, they only accentuated it. Now, as he fixed Lars with that sudden beady-eyed stare, the gnomelike features became somehow macabre. "It appears that you made an error during crew ident, Mr. Clemens."

Lars felt a surge of adrenaline. An error? He forced his hands apart, placing his palms flat against the padded arms of his chair. An *error?* "Sir?"

"Cracchiolo," Spick barked. "You missed his name during crew identification."

"I noticed that," Spalding interjected, a little too quickly.

"What about it?" Spick snapped.

Lars licked lips that were suddenly dry. His stomach tightened. "Reception was a bit scratchy, sir. It's true that I missed Vito Cracchiolo's name during final crew ident, but I checked it on my roster—"

"Commbox reception was poor?" Spick's eyes darted over the transcript sheets, waving them in the air as he looked from one to the other. "I don't see any mention of commbox reception being poor."

"Neither did I," Spalding began.

"Shut up," Spick snapped. Spalding drew back as if he'd been stung. "What about it, Clemens?"

"I didn't think it was necessary to report that, sir—"

"You didn't think it was necessary to report it," Spick mimicked. He leaned back in his chair, the tips of his fingers arching together to form a bridge through which he looked at Lars. "Why did you take it upon yourself to make that decision, Mr. Clemens?"

"Because—" Lars's voice faltered. He swallowed, drew a breath, and started over. "The reception was no better nor worse than it usually is. We often have static—"

"Nor did you consider the problem of crew ident of sufficient substance to mention."

Lars's mind reeled under the barrage. He worked to keep his voice steady. "That's true, sir. It didn't seem relevant at the time. As I said, I checked the roster—"

"I know what you said, Mr. Clemens. It's what you have *not* said that concerns me." Spick waved the transcript sheets. "It's what you decided not to mention because of your personal values regarding relevancy that I want to know about."

"There's nothing else, sir."

"Nothing?" Spick fixed him with a how-can-we-be-sure-of-that stare. *"Nothing?"*

Lars gave Spalding a quick look, hoping for support. They had covered all this before coming to Spick, and Spalding had been in total agreement that all procedures concerning McElroy's skip had been followed to the letter. But the CommSec Assistant Director's attention seemed to be focused on a silver paperweight—a miniature *Graywand*—on Spick's desk.

"My report," Lars said at last, "is as complete as I know how to make it, sir."

"Yes, I'm sure it is," Spick said with acid politeness. "With all the *relevant* facts."

Lars kept silent. This time he did not allow his eyes to fall away from Spick's.

"How long have you been in CommSec?" Spick asked suddenly.

"Six months, sir."

Spick stared at him a moment longer, then turned away abruptly to place the transcript in the top drawer of his desk. "I can't take this to Captain Uriah until we know more about what happened. Sounds like a NavSec problem to me. Let's get the facts together." A quick glance was flung at Lars. "*All* the facts. Then we'll determine CommSec's exposure."

Spalding stood. The meeting was over. Lars rose hastily, nearly bumping into his superior.

"Exactly what I was going to suggest," Spalding said. "We'll let you know later today if we find anything."

"I'll be leaving for *Ysola* in twenty minutes. I'll be there for the rest of today and most of tomorrow." Spick withdrew another report from his desk and opened it in front of him.

"Fine. We'll, uh, get back to you later."

Spick made no reply. His attention was on the opened report. Lars and Spalding exited quietly through the door into the narrow corridor outside.

"Let's go through the transcript again," Spalding said. He seemed pleased with the way the meeting had gone. "I want to be sure we haven't missed anything."

"We've been through it a dozen times." Lars felt the words coming out of him before he could stop them. "We aren't going to find anything new. We'll only waste more time—" He bit off his words. Getting Spalding upset would solve nothing.

But Spalding seemed not to notice. "You're probably right. But the man," he jerked a thumb toward Spick's office, "wants us to look." They stepped into an elevator, and Lars pressed the lighted square for the second level. Spalding reached past him and pressed for the seventh. "I'll be at the Cornucopia if anything comes up."

Lars stood in dumbfounded silence as the doors hissed open a moment later and Spalding stepped out.

"I don't get it," Lars said to Carl Lunsford as he sank wearily into his chair. "We have to get NavSec working on this. We've got to find out what happened. Spick doesn't seem to be interested in doing anything."

"Sure he is," Lunsford replied. "He's interested in making sure his hindquarters are covered in case this turns out to be serious."

"In case it turns out to be serious?" Lars echoed in amazement. "Five people are lost. We don't know where they are, and we've lost contact with them. Isn't that serious enough?"

Lunsford shrugged. He was working with his control board, setting up an approaching skip cycle. "Serious enough to get people in trouble. Spick wants to make sure he isn't trapped in the pot when the water begins to boil. By calling in NavSec he'll be admitting the problem exists. There'll be no turning back after that."

Lars shook his head. "That line of reasoning makes no sense to me."

"That's why Spick's the director and we're the hired help," Lunsford pointed out. "He can reason things out to fit whatever conclusion he needs, while we have to be satisfied with looking at the facts. Besides, the last thing he wants is to screw up his chances for the Omega job."

Lars looked over at Lunsford. "Omega job?"

"Kelly's retiring next month." Alvin Kelly was central communications officer for Omega, stationed at the administrative offices on Noura. "Word has it that Spick's one of the front runners for the spot. He doesn't want anybody bringing up questions about his work here, especially not with the selection committee meeting tomorrow."

"On *Ysola*," Lars murmured. Lunsford was right, he was sure of it. Spick was stalling.

"What?"

"The committee meeting. That must be it. On *Ysola*. Spick's going over there today."

Lunsford shrugged and said nothing, his eyes on the readout screen.

Lars leaned forward and propped his elbows on the console shelf, steepling his hands under his chin. He sat that way for a long moment, then sighed resignedly and entered a command into his control board. The console printer hummed briefly and spit out another yellow copy of his coordination dialogue with McElroy. He tore it off and went through it again, line by line.

After thirty minutes he knew he was wasting his time. There was nothing wrong with the confirmations between McElroy and himself, nothing to even suggest an error in the authorization provided by *Graywand*'s navigator.

"We've got to call in the navigation techs," he muttered again, staring at the furled transcript sheet. He shifted his gaze to Lunsford. "We have to find out what happened before it's too late."

"It's out of your hands." Lunsford turned to look directly at Lars, his tone serious. "You've turned it over to Spick. It's his responsibility. If you're thinking of going around him, you'd better think again. You're asking for trouble."

"He isn't doing anything."

"Without his authority, how can *you* hope to accomplish anything?"

Lunsford posed a question for which Lars had no answer. A commclerk could hardly hope to initiate an inquiry without the CommSec Director's support.

"Look," Lunsford continued, "whatever happened isn't your fault. You did everything right. And you've reported it to Spick himself. You're off the hook. Why stick your neck out farther?"

Another question that had no easy answer. What had happened to McElroy and the others was not the result of an error on Lars's part. But that did little to ease his feeling of responsibility. Lars had set up the skip, and he'd been the last person to speak with McElroy. It had been to Lars, not to Spalding or Spick or Carl Lunsford, that McElroy had pleaded for an immediate return to *Graywand*.

That's the wind. Sixty knots, at least.

One doubt nagged at Lars above all others: Had he done everything he could for McElroy and the others? When McElroy called to say they had broken out in the wrong place, had he looked at every possible option for getting them back? He'd been convinced at the time that he had, but he realized now that when that last call came, he had been so caught up in the hows and whys of what had happened that the task of expediting the audit crew's return took an almost secondary position. He had not seriously considered that they might be in danger, had not given a thought to the possibility of losing contact with McElroy. He'd reworked the schedule to provide what he believed to be the earliest break in the cycle. But had he looked closely enough? Could he have done better? When all was said and done, had his reactions been any better than those of Robert Spalding and Raymond Spick?

"Can you cover for me, Carl?" he asked suddenly.

"Sure, but—"

"I'm going up to NavSec." Lars rolled the yellow transcript into a tube and stood up. "It shouldn't take long."

"You're looking to get bounced right off *Graywand*, Lars."

"I'll try to keep my questions unofficial," Lars promised.

Lunsford grunted. "You bring up something like this, it'll be hard to keep it unofficial." He paused, looking at Lars. "You know Benjamin Hill?"

Lars thought for a moment, then shook his head.

"He's a systems tech in NavSec," Lunsford said. "One of the best. He may be able to help you. Tell him the Snake sent you."

"The snake?"

"He'll understand."

CHAPTER SIX

McElroy stared in disbelief at the row of green lights above the console. His eyes moved to the switch, now lighted, under the thrown-back safety cover. "This isn't possible," he said softly.

"What?" Vikki Redford demanded loudly. "What did you say?"

McElroy made no reply. Sand pinged against the outside of the pod. The cooling unit hummed steadily. McElroy looked up at the vidscreens—the barren valley, the distant forest, the rocky knoll behind them. With a slight shake of his head he leaned forward and reset the final stages of skip sequence, then pressed the blue button again. Nothing happened. The readout screen said: DRIVE SYSTEM READY.

Drive system ready—

Behind him, Vikki Redford asked another question. He ignored her and keyed in another command:

55

STATUS CHECK

The screen flashed: READY...

McElroy entered: DRIVE SYSTEM

WHAT? asked the brain.

He steadied himself and thought for a moment, then tried again:

CHECK DRIVE SYSTEM INTEGRITY
WHAT?

"Damnation!" he exploded. "Do we have a manual around here for this thing?"

"I'll take a look, cap'n," Cracchiolo answered quickly.

McElroy stared at the screen, calming himself. Then he tried a new approach:

SYSTEMS CHECK
READY...
DRIVE ENGINE
DO YOU WANT OPERATIONAL CHECK
OF ENTIRE DRIVE SYSTEM?

McElroy jabbed his reply viciously into the control pad: YES

Jack-a-dandy went to work. The wind kicked up, jostling the tiny craft. The sounder blipped in its niche in the corner. Behind him he heard Cracchiolo rustling through drawers. A throat was cleared. Someone coughed uneasily. Figures rippled across the screen.

DRIVE SYSTEM CHECK COMPLETED
READY...

The drive engines were okay. Thank God for that, he thought. Or thank whatever deity lurked over this unholy place. He entered the word SPUD.

WHAT?
COMMUTATOR

Jack-a-dandy took a moment to digest this vague request,
then asked:

DO YOU WANT OPERATIONAL CHECK
OF KOHLMANN STREAM COMMUTATOR?

"Oh, for—" He jabbed at the control pad: YES.
The pause was very brief this time.

MALFUNCTION IN R-WAVE RELAY SYSTEM
OF KOHLMANN STREAM COMMUTATOR
EXAMINE AND CORRECT
READY . . .

"Doesn't leave much doubt, cap'n," Cracchiolo said
after a moment. "The spud isn't working."

"I know that," McElroy snapped. "*Why* isn't it
working?"

"Bad connection?" Stone suggested.

"Can't be," Cracchiolo said flatly. "Triple backup on
everything. Fail-safe. One circuit might blow, but not all
three. Even *our* luck can't be that bad."

"Can't it?" Vikki asked wryly.

McElroy knew how she felt. One problem after another
stacking up on their shoulders, and the feeling of being
stranded growing with each moment. It was not something
that fit into their comfortably packaged lives.

"Can we fix it?" Wheeler asked.

Cracchiolo's silence was answer enough. Sand rattled
against the outside of the pod, driven by another stray gust
of wind.

McElroy drew a breath. "Crackers," he ordered tersely,
"you and Stone dig the spud out. Take a look at the
connections, see if you can spot the trouble."

Cracchiolo looked up in surprise. "Take the spud out?"

"That's what I said."

"It's built right into the drive assembly, cap'n."

"I didn't say it would be easy. I just said do it. Check the circuits while you're in there. All three sets. If there's a short, find it."

"We aren't mechanics—" Stone began.

"That's right." McElroy snapped. "We're accountants. And we are going to be dead accountants if we don't get the drive system fixed and get out of this place."

Cracchiolo and Stone exchanged glances. Then, without another word, they went to the supply bin at the rear of the pod and began looking through it for usable tools. McElroy returned once again to the corner chair, his heart thudding uncomfortably in his chest. *It's getting to me too*, he thought.

A half hour passed. The cooling unit began to whine and rattle, laboring against the building heat. Cracchiolo and Stone struggled with inadequate tools to disassemble the drive system components. Wheeler sat at the counter, looking up at the vidscreens. Vikki sat beside him, looking angry. McElroy leaned his head back against the chair, feeling drained by the heat.

"Excuse me, Oliver. I think we're forgetting something."

McElroy's head lifted slowly and turned toward Wheeler. He hated it when people called him Oliver.

"Perhaps we should give ourselves some alternatives," Wheeler went on. "In case we don't get the drive system fixed right away. I imagine we'll see a rather severe drop in temperature at nightfall. That's common in an arid environment."

"So?" McElroy lacked the energy to trace through Wheeler's convoluted thought patterns.

"Heat exchange," Wheeler explained. "Rapid temperature changes can result in substantial air convection. If the wind we've seen is any indication of what we may face later, we could be in trouble."

A valid point, McElroy had to admit. But he was irritated that Wheeler had been the one to think of it. "What are you suggesting?"

"If we're in for more wind, the pod may not be a safe place to spend the night. I'd like to go out and look around, see if I can find more secure shelter if we need it."

A typical Wheeler nuttyism, McElroy thought. If they were unable to repair the spud by nightfall, they would not be getting it repaired at all. He opened his mouth to tell Wheeler to forget it, then he looked at Wheeler's pale eyes and hesitated.

When McElroy was a kid, in those good years on Terra when he and his father used to go camping in the cool hills above the city of Sacramento, they had once come across a young cottontail caught in a trapper's snare. The cottontail had mangled its hind leg trying to get free. When the boy approached, morbidly drawn to the pain and blood, the young rabbit rolled its eyes up at him. He had never in his life seen a creature so full of desperation and hopelessness. He remembered that young cottontail now as he looked at Wheeler's gray eyes.

The past few hours had touched something inside John Wheeler. Wheeler was a quiet man by nature—exasperatingly so at times. He rarely responded to others, doing so only when forced to it by a direct question. He had revealed little of his past to McElroy in the three years they had known one another. Now, seeing in those pale eyes a kind of desperation that spoke so quietly of fear and pain, McElroy realized that something about this planet was triggering a reaction deep inside Wheeler. Wheeler was pleading. And really, McElroy decided, the man had a point about the need for shelter. The pod would not survive a night of high winds on this rock ledge.

"All right," he said curtly. "Look around, if you want to. But stay close to the pod."

A brief smile of gratitude flickered across Wheeler's face. A moment later the desert sucked the last of the cool air out of the pod as the hatchcover creaked open and Wheeler stepped out onto the scorched ground.

CHAPTER SEVEN

Wheeler had expected, from what he'd seen in the limited view provided by *jack-a-dandy*'s vidscreen, that the forest would be as harsh and ugly as the trees scattered across the valley floor—burned black by the blazing sun, frozen in an agony of deformed growth. But as he left the brown-baked sand and entered the first belt of forest, he saw instead somber tones of red and purple, misshapen limbs crowding close together in a kind of fluidity that gave strength and substance, not dark ugliness. The glare of the sun filtered through as a soft glow, a welcome relief to eyes punished by the glare of the valley floor.

Wheeler stopped inside this first line of trees and tested the earth with the toe of his boot. Small skittering sounds and rustlings reminded him of the high-plain woodlands of Kahliyl, where he'd spent many years as a young man. This planet, harsh as it was, nurtured life. Perhaps even intelligents. He smiled at that thought. An audit crew landing a planet with gents. That would turn a few heads.

He stood for a moment, taking in the alien scents and sounds, enjoying the relative cool of the forest. It had seemed only natural to come toward the forest. If shelter from the wind were to be found, it would be here, not on the bald mound of rock behind the pod, and not in the barren valley. They would be safe here in the forest with the strange trees humming in the wind and murmuring life-sounds all around them.

He smiled faintly and, as if to reassure himself, turned to look back the way he'd come—the desert burned under the white heat of the sun, the pod a dark speck against the chalk-white ledge a kilometer or more away. He was surprised to see that he'd covered no more distance than that. The desert, the pod, the people inside it—they seemed an eternity away from the dark sanctity of the forest.

He turned slowly back to the forest's quiet presence, listening.

There was more to it than a mass of trees and scrubby undergrowth. There was something else—more than the scuttling sounds of tiny creatures and the moan of the wind through high, twisted branches and the scent of mossy growth, more than the natural sounds and smells of this unnatural place.

He stood waiting, shivering as he felt it again: an alien presence inside his mind, touching him, scurrying away, then returning for another brief touch. He listened, straining, almost imagining that he could hear a thin whispery voice calling his name, almost feeling a sensation like that of returning home after a long absence.

"Nonsense." But the word came as a question, not a statement. He swallowed, and almost imagined that faint murmur urging him on. He'd felt it from the moment Oliver McElroy had activated the vidscreens and he had looked out on that strange, barren world. He'd felt that— *presence* inside him, just at the edge of perception.

"Nonsense," he said again, louder this time, and struck off through the trees. He did not think of the distance he was placing between himself and the pod, or consider for even a moment the possibility of danger there in the strange, dark forest. He strode ahead under the canopy of twisted branches, breathed the scents of growth around him, and did not even stop to think where he was going. He picked his way through thorny clumps of vegetation, stepped across an occasional bony outgrowth of rock, and glanced upwards now and then.

The shadowy forest ended as abruptly as it had begun, and Wheeler stood facing the burning desert once more. Ahead of him the sand sloped gently down toward the ruins of an ancient city.

Wheeler stood for a long moment at the edge of the forest, taking it in. It was a vision to be taken whole, a mosaic of expression rather than a group of details, an outgrowth of the desert, tones of rust-red and brown and cream formed into blocks and spheres and curved spires and fragments of bone-white latticework hanging like fragile nets from slender towers. Erosion had mellowed it all, bringing it into subtle harmony with the desert. It was an outgrowth of time and wind and sand, a product of those three gods.

I've been here before, he thought suddenly, looking down at the city. Then, confused, he shook his head. *No, that isn't possible.* He looked out at the city and felt other eyes looking out at it with him. The feeling was too strong to deny. He remembered the city as one remembers the place of one's childhood, forms and shadows altered by time—the perception of the child changed by intervening years to that of an adult.

Childhood—

Wheeler's mind tumbled back through fifty years, touching here a bright moment of happiness, settling there on a frozen instant of pain, flipping with equal agility through vague shapes and needle-sharp detail, passing randomly through the long corridors of his past. For the moment of a heartbeat: Growing up in East Chicago, the sixty-first-floor apartment, slipcars moving below like tiny colored beetles along the transtube of Westchester Drive—a river of them flowing together, blending their colors as instruments of music blend random sound into a symphony. Yes, this ancient city of the blazing sand was like music, the motions of a poem gathered into a single unit, a sigh. The city: It was real to him, preserved through time, not an empty vision at all.

Wheeler breathed the dry air, felt the white heat burning down on his exposed neck, and thought how utterly perfect and in place the city looked there on the desert floor. It had been built by those who knew beauty and peace, who knew how to fit themselves into their world with grace. In comparison, the cities of humankind were crude and vulgar.

Again came the fleeting alien touch. He cocked his head, listening. Memories tumbled.

Age twelve: After an especially frustrating session with the piano, his mother telling him over and over that he had to try harder. Her voice tight and bitter, full of disappointment. He was destined for mediocrity, like his father— and John Wheeler understood that she referred to all of him, not merely to the part that wrenched clumsy notes from the piano.

He blinked, and the ghost from the past faded. A sigh whispered out of him. He drew a breath, released it. Then he started down the slope toward the nearest of the block structures.

Thirty minutes later, his head swimming from the heat, he rested in the shade of a low building with truncated corners and a single white spire curving upwards a hundred meters or more from one side. The walls were made of large stones, squared and finely cut for a close fit. One large section had crumbled, revealing an interior that was utterly bare. He'd searched through half a dozen of the broken buildings, breathed the hot dry air, left his footprints in the drifted sand, listened to the heavy silence— and found in all of them nothing but depressing emptiness.

He forced himself to breathe evenly while the dizziness and the throbbing in his temples subsided. He eased himself into a more comfortable position, wincing as a sharp sciatic pain lanced through his leg.

I'm too old for this, he told himself. *Much too old*.

He stared into the wavering heat shimmer and felt the hot sand under him and thought, *All my life I've done nothing but wish for better days. Other men have done big things, while I have only dreamed. Through all the long years— always the dreams of wanting, and not knowing what. Years of empty visions, wasted years. And what single satisfying goal have I reached?*

The dead city waited under the sun-glazed air.

He closed his eyes and felt the questioning touch. His mind moved back fifty years to another day: A young boy, standing on a balcony in the cold hard hours before dawn while a freezing norther swept across the lake whipping his thin pajamas against his frail body. Folded in his trembling hands was a steel air-sculpture, the most fragile and beautiful object he had ever created with those two hands— hands that were utterly worthless when it came to ordinary tasks like swinging a bat or catching a football or playing the piano. He had wrought this sculpture from a solid bar of steel, breathed life into it for his mother—to make up in a small way for all his faults and failings. His mother considered the flowing silver strands, the webbed base— this perfect offering from her imperfect son—and remarked that she preferred realism in her art. Abstraction, she asserted, was the product of a vague mind.

With the icy wind full in his face, he raised the sculpture and flung it out into the black night, watching as it fell silently like a drop of rain into the lighted pond at the base of the tower. He stared down at the tiny ripples of water for a long time, picturing in his mind the effect a larger object would have had on that placid pond.

Now, opening his eyes to look out at the silent city, Wheeler realized that the night in East Chicago so many years ago had been a time of purging for him. His unworthiness, his inability to please the one person that mattered to him—that supreme being who established good and evil and judged his accomplishments with an omniscient eye—all these failings required a sacrifice of hope. His father's sacrifice was much greater—the turning of a man of ideals and values into an uncaring alcoholic.

Illusion—his life, the city, the empty years—all made of visions and fears.

And sand.

Wheeler laughed out loud. He looked up,. startled to hear the sound of his own laughter rattling through the dead city.

It was all for this, he thought suddenly. The growing-up years, the wandering years, the wanting years—all designed for the single purpose of bringing him to this city. Each moment of longing, each failing—mere stepping stones to this place, molding him to a certain form for a certain purpose. Even Cari, yes even she had been only a prelude.

"No," he said aloud.

Yes, whispered a voice inside him.

He squinted up into a high curving spire, feeling the ancient strength sifting down through the years.

For you, whispered the voice.

He knew this city. Not its intimate details—not the way a person who had grown up in a city would know it—but he knew its design, knew how its builders had put it together for protection against wind, drifting dust, scouring sand. He knew of the underground passages that once bound it together. He knew of the spirit of life that had been with its builders.

Yes, he knew this city.

He sat there a moment longer, feeling the hot breath of the city all around him. And suddenly, for no reason, he was afraid.

He pushed himself to his feet, and a bolt of sciatic agony lanced up through his leg. He winced, leaned against the wall to steady himself, and felt the creeping sensation of that other presence inside, sharing the pain.

Cari—

A cottage in the green woods of Kahliyl. The girl, Cari,

with flowing hair and eyes so deep and green that looking
into them made him feel weak. A summer stroll through
blackberries and hazel, sharing love in the tall, soft grass.
Cari. He had not thought of her in years. Looking back
now, he wondered if even she had been illusion. Could
anything so free and beautiful be real? Not for Wheeler.
Not even then, at twenty years of age, with that dead
specter from the past a constant companion, a scornful
reminder of his unworthiness.

The older Wheeler, hunched against the stone wall,
breathing the dust and heat and looking back on those
decades, understood what had been well beyond the comprehension of that younger self caught in the trap set so
cleverly by his mother. She had left a legacy of hate for
her son, whom she had indeed hated. She had set the trap,
baited it, and called him in; and that younger, unknowing
Wheeler had entered willingly, never to escape. The trap—
his unworthiness, his inability to accept warmth and life
from others—had taken him whole. Cari had been the
supreme test of the ghost's power. She had brought John
Wheeler out of his self-made desolation with her love and
patience. She had understood his fears, and with unselfish
caring had drawn aside the cloak of illusion to let Wheeler
see for the first time the world and his place in it.

But the ghost's influence was strong. Little by little,
Cari drew away, as did all those others who tried to come
close to John Wheeler. She touched him and felt the
coldness and drew back. He'd gone through his life that
way, feeling them draw away, and never in all those years
of wanting only a touch of affection had he been able to
accept that touch when it came. Like the scrubby plants in
the Terran deserts, plants that spread poison about them to
prevent seedlings from growing too close in the continuing
fight for survival in a harsh environment, Wheeler had
spread coldness throughout his life.

Looking back, the memory of Cari was especially painful. Somehow, with the blazing city all around him and his
mind touched by the presence of those who had built it, he

could see himself with painful clarity. Gentle Cari. He had separated himself from her, had purposefully set out to destroy the beauty they'd shared for the simple reason that a ghost from the past had whispered that he was undeserving of it. He had given up so much when he gave up Cari, and all through his life he had rejected all that might have made him happy.

He looked out at the city and shook his head. *Am I going insane?*

He turned, anxious now to get back to the pod—and stiffened as his eyes traced a path between two ruined structures. In the distance, he saw a tomb.

That it was a tomb was obvious to him. A large structure, vastly different from anything else he had seen in the city. Parts of it had crumbled into ruin, but for the most part it was intact—a great, hulking five-sided edifice rising well above the others around it.

He stared for a long moment, breath rasping in and out of him, and thought, *This is what I came here to find. Not the city. Only this single piece of it: The tomb.*

Yes, whispered the voice inside him.

He faced into the hot wind and walked over heat-crackling sand toward the hulking ruin.

CHAPTER EIGHT

"Carl Lunsford? Ha! He ever tell you about the Parelli fiasco?"

"Not that I remember—"

"Snake. That's what we call him. Lunsford will go after anything that's female. Anything." Benjamin Hill hunched over a workbench that was cluttered with tools and instruments and a disassembled something that Lars thought might once have been a relay element. Hill was a large man, with rounded shoulders, an unfashionably shaggy beard, and long hair gathered in a bun at the nape of his neck. He worked with the quick precision that comes with intimate knowledge of tools and machinery. "Lunsford got what he deserved on Parelli, that's for sure."

Lars dropped into a hard plastic chair beside the workbench—one of *Graywand*'s so-called "utility" chairs that had been designed for durability, ease of storage, and maximum discomfort. "Why is he called Snake?"

"Cause he's got—" Hill looked up suddenly, then grinned

and went back to his work. "Better let him tell you that one."

"The two of you must go back a ways."

"Yes," Hill agreed, snatching up a wrench, working briefly with it, flinging it down. "A ways, for sure."

"Carl says you're the resident expert on the navigation system."

"I know my way around it," Hill admitted. His fingers worked at the element with a small screwdriver. "You need info?"

"Well—"

"And you don't want to go through official channels." Teeth flashed through the beard. "No problem. Always figured, if we could get rid of the puking bureaucrats, we'd get the job done in half the time. Fire away."

"Thanks. I was wondering—"

A handset buzzed at the corner of the desk. Hill snatched it up and listened a moment, making a series of long-suffering explanatory faces at Lars. "Can't talk now, babe. Call me back in half an hour." He banged the handset into its cradle, plucked the screwdriver from the workbench, and nodded for Lars to resume.

"The k-stream coordinates," Lars went on, slightly off-balance. "They seem to be the key to the navigator. I work with them all the time, but I'm not even sure what they are. How can a set of simple numbers pinpoint a location in the stream?"

"They can't. All they do is tell the navigator how to tell itself how to make the skip." Another quick grin. "Navigator's pretty puking stupid when you come right down to it. You know how the stream works?"

"Not really."

"Most people don't. That's why they don't understand the coordinates. They work with a bunch of numbers, give them to a navigation computer that does something mystical with them, and nobody cares how it all works—so long as it all works. Slaves to our own creations, that's what we are." Hill's voice quickened as he expanded on a subject that was obviously dear to him. He finished with the screwdriver and tugged away a piece of the element with fingers that were surprisingly gentle. "You hit the nail smack on the head. How can you describe a planet's location with a half-dozen numbers? What *is* a planet's location? Location has no meaning unless you describe it as a relationship to something else. Right?"

"Well—"

"That's not half of it when it comes to the stream. Stream relationships don't have anything whatever to do with spatial relationships. Spatially, you and I are sitting here maybe a meter apart, but the Kohlmann stream doesn't see it that way. We may not even be in the same skip zone in the stream. Point is, it makes no sense to describe a planet in the stream as being near this one or far from this one or just around 'he corner from that one. The stream doesn't work that way. That's what's so remarkable about it. And it's why the navigator can do what it does."

"Because," Lars said, "the coordinates tell it how."

Hill blinked. He stared at Lars for a moment, then grinned. "I do tend to go on at times. It's just that, well, once you work out all this for yourself, it's like you realized you were dead before and just came to life." He paused for a moment, looking down at the relay element in his hands, collecting his thoughts. Then he placed the element on the workbench and turned to Lars, folding his hands across his stomach. "*Graywand* is a fixed point in the stream. No particular reason—she's stationary simply because we've said she is. Anything moving to or from *Graywand* can be described in terms of that fixed point. As long as the navigator knows where *Graywand* is, sending something to another point in the stream is only a matter of correlating the stream maneuvers with balance measurements and othersuch and sending them to the drive system. The drive engines form the insulating field, work through the stream maneuvers in something under a millisecond, and poof you're there." He paused, studying the bewildered look on Lars's face. "The point is, the navigator doesn't have to work out all that stuff each time it cycles a skip. Takes a lot of brain power to do that, so it's only done once. When the planet's first cataloged.''

"Cataloged?"

"Right. When Field Recon lands the planet. Stream maneuvers are boiled down and filed in the navigator's own registers. Everything it needs, all the stream maneuvers and balances are right there for it to use. All it has to do is reach in and get them, run correlation checks through hardwired Kohlmann functions, and feed them to the drive system of the breakout vessel.''

"And the coordinates—"

Hill spread his large hands, palms up. "They tell it where to go in its own files for what it needs." He seemed delighted that he'd finally gotten the idea across. "They're really nothing more than the navigator's own file system."

"Could they be wrong?"

"Wrong?" The expression of delight crumpled. "How could they be wrong?"

Lars shrugged. "Coordinates assigned to the wrong planet, maybe—one planet getting mixed up with another in the navigator's file—"

"No way." Hill shook his head vigorously. "Too many counter-checks. The navigator's set up to look for errors before it gives the okay for a skip." The handset buzzed again. Hill gave it a dark look and snatched it up. "Go away." He slammed it down. "Internal consistency and all that," he said to Lars. "The navigator has to know it's been given a legitimate stream location before it'll go ahead with the skip."

Lars suddenly remembered something Rod Clawson had told him: *A few weeks ago we had a Blue drop in here by mistake. It happens now and then.*

"But there are errors sometimes, aren't there?"

Hill waved his hand in dismissal. "One per every fifty thousand skips, maybe. But they're never because of the navigator. Never. Someone gives it whacky coordinates, someone provides whacky authorization. Sure, it'll okay a skip to the wrong target. It can't read minds." Hill spun in his chair and reached for a cup from a shelf behind him. He looked into it with a grimace, then drew some jo from a portable dispenser. "We can probably scare up another cup."

"None for me, thanks. You were saying about bad skips?"

"Not bad skips. Bad coordinates. The navigator can check itself, but it can't verify the smart-power of the idiots that give it information." An aroma of spice drifted from the cup as Hill leaned back in his chair and sipped noisily. "Human error, that's where the trouble is whenever there's a bad skip. If it gets the right coordinates, the navigator will do what it's supposed to do."

Human error. The search for the answer always came back to doubts about Lars's confirmation of coordinates. "Is there any way," he asked, "for the stored information—the k-stream maneuvers, you called them—to be wrong?"

Again came the exaggerated back-and-forth movement of Hill's head. "They stick with the target from the time of first landing by Field Recon. The characteristics are logged in, and the coordinates are set up at the same time. From then on they never change."

Human error. Find the key. The coordinates he and McElroy had gone through were without fault. Lars had been through them enough times to be sure. So the human error lay elsewhere. "Could Field Recon make a mistake setting up the coordinates?"

"Sure," Hill conceded easily. "But the Blue would catch it. Checks and double checks, remember? Before the coordinates are filed permanently with the navigator, the Blue sends a drone through the stream to the target planet. Then they shoot it a message. If the drone answers, they know it got through okay. A Blue makes a real skip as a final test. Coordinates aren't released for general use until all this is cleared. If there was going to be a problem, it'd show up then." Teeth flashed under the beard. "You see, we've got it covered from all angles."

* * *

It happens now and then. A few weeks ago we had a Blue pop in here by mistake.

Rod Clawson had made that statement to Lars only a few hours ago. And another statement by Benjamin Hill: *A Blue makes the initial skip.*

The two statements came together in a way that made Lars aware of something he had not yet considered. Nearly all the initial work of a newly landed planet was done by the Blue. The link was there. The Blue: that elite group within Field Recon that was responsible for setting up survey posts, for making first contact with intelligents, for making hostile environments suitable for humans. The Blue was always first on the scene, professionals trained in a hundred special fields to perform UNSA's most dangerous work.

Human error.

Something had gone wrong. Benjamin Hill was mistaken in his assurances. Not every angle had been covered. Something had gone askew, and Lars had to find it.

He leaned across the console and entered the coordinates for the Sierra post.

"Mr. Clawson? This is Lars Clemens."

"Yeah, kid," rasped the voice in Lars's headset. "Find your missing auditors?"

"Not yet, sir. You mentioned earlier about someone who broke out on Sierra by mistake?"

"Yeah?"

"You said he was a Blue—"

"She. Arrogant bitch, too. Acted like it was my fault she skipped to the wrong place. Has a real chip on her shoulder, if you ask me."

"Any idea how it might have happened?"

"Sure. Parents banged her around as a kid. Grew up bitter and resentful, takes it out on everyone she meets."

"No, Mr. Clawson. I meant the breakout on Sierra."

Clawson's laughter rattled Lars's headset, making him wince. "Just putting you on, kid. Sure, I know how it happened. She gave the navigator the wrong coordinates. That's what I told her.''

"But she was Blue—"

"I know what you're thinking, kid. But they ain't gods. They can screw up just like the rest of us. I told her that, too. Don't think she cared much for it.''

"Do you remember her name, sir?"

"I never asked for it. She wasn't my type, anyway. Not by a long shot.''

"Do you have any idea how I can find her?"

"You wouldn't want to, believe me. Listen, kid, I got a lot of papers growing on my desk. You got anything else?''

Lars sat motionless, his eyes fixed on a point just above the glowing green light of the commbox. The link was here. It had to be.

"Thanks, Mr. Clawson."

"Any time, kid."

Lars clicked off and leaned back in his chair, trying to put his thoughts in order. McElroy and his crew had not reached Sierra. But the navigation computer confirmed Sierra coordinates prior to the skip, which made no sense, because if the navigator confirmed coordinates to Sierra, then those same coordinates should have taken McElroy there. Errors are the result of sloppiness. Neither McElroy nor Lars had been sloppy in setting up the skip.

Human error. A Blue had mistakenly skipped to Sierra. Something Benjamin Hill said earlier: The navigator could not read minds. It had only the facts it was given.

Which came down to one conclusion: Someone had given the navigator bad data. And the link was a skip to Sierra by a Blue who thought she was going somewhere else. If the skip had gone bad in one direction, had it also gone bad in the other? The Blue had given a set of coordinates to *Graywand*'s navigator and found herself on Sierra. She had expected to go somewhere else.

Somewhere else.

Perhaps to confirm coordinates for a newly landed planet.

Somewhere else.

Where?

CHAPTER NINE

Metal surfaces inside the pod had become too hot to touch. The air was heat-heavy and suffocating. The cooling unit had groaned terribly and given up the battle an hour earlier.

Oliver McElroy slumped in the corner chair, feeling drained and boneless. It was hell outside, even in the small pool of shade cast by the ledge. But it was worse in here. The pod was an oven, soaking up the sun's heat and concentrating it in the tiny cabin.

"Anybody know the kindling point of the human body?" he asked.

Vito Cracchiolo chuckled a reply that McElroy missed. Cracchiolo seemed impervious to the heat. He lay on his back under the console, arms stretched up into the control system's inner workings, legs sprawled out across the floor amid tools and pieces of the control system. Tom Stone sat melting in a corner.

"Brother Thomas," Cracchiolo called out cheerily, "do you see a number ten spanner out there?"

Stone stirred and looked around groggily. He leaned forward with a grunt, plucked a wrench out of the litter on the floor, and placed it in Cracchiolo's waiting hand.

"Think you'll be able to get it back together?" McElroy wiped a stinging rivulet of sweat out of his eye and thought, *How can he work in here?*

"Faith, cap'n. We got every nut and bolt committed to memory. Right, Brother Thomas?" Stone made an unintelligible sound. Something snapped under the console, and another piece came tumbling out. "John show up yet?"

"Not yet." Vikki Redford was still out there, watching from the shade of the rock ledge in case Wheeler appeared.

"Stop fretting, cap'n. John's wearing a sounder. He'll find his way back. Like Ma used to say about us boys, 'He'll come back when he gets hungry.' "

He'd better, McElroy said to himself, *or I'll leave him here*. But he knew he wouldn't. If it came to it, they could track Wheeler down. The sounder on Wheeler's wrist, a standard-issue tracking device tied into a homing unit in the pod, would lead them to him. McElroy glanced at the chronometer and placed his palms flat on the arms of the chair, stilling the urge inside his fingers to tap the one-two-three rhythm on the hard plastic. He'd give Wheeler another fifteen minutes. A flurry of sand rattled against the pod, and McElroy thought, *Ought to go back out there and make sure Vikki's okay*.

But still he sat there in the heavy heat, nurturing his doubts. What if Wheeler was right? What if *Graywand* couldn't find them? What if they'd broken out on some planet that wasn't even charted yet?

Before that unhappy thought could go any further, Vikki Redford poked her head through the hatchway and said, "Wheeler's coming."

A moment later McElroy scrambled down the crumbling ledge to stand beside her, watching as the distant figure came toward them across the sand.

*   *   *

"What were you thinking, John? I want to know. What prompted you to take a three-hour jaunt when you said you'd be gone fifteen minutes?"

John Wheeler shrugged his thin shoulders and looked down at his hands. He sat on a cargo mat someone had dragged out of *jack-a-dandy*'s supply hold and spread within the narrow bar of shade from the ledge. He leaned back against the red stone and rubbed one bony knuckle with a thumb.

"It isn't enough," McElroy stormed, standing over him, "that we're stuck in this godforsaken place with a dead drive system. You have to go wandering off on your own, just take off; and maybe someone goes looking for you and they don't come back either; and someone else goes looking, and before you know it we're all wandering around like blind mice looking for each other. God's name, John, what were you thinking? What possessed you to do such a thing?"

Wheeler lifted his shoulders again. Then, as if knowing that the passive shrug would only fuel McElroy's wrath, he looked up and blurted, "There's a city out there, Oliver. A big one."

McElroy was taken up short. "A city?"

Wheeler's head bobbed up and down. "Just on the other side of those trees. So beautiful it makes you ache, looking at it."

"Intelligents," Vikki murmured beside him.

"Not anymore. The city's old, mostly in ruins. No intelligent life around that I could see. But there's something else. A tomb of some sort, like nothing I've ever seen. And, Oliver, I can't help but wonder what's inside. It's like a—" He stopped abruptly, seeming to realize that he was beginning to babble. His thin lips closed tightly, and his hand went to the bronze amulet at his throat. "I needed to see it, that's all."

"You needed to see it," McElroy repeated with an acid tone. "Let me tell you something, John. At this moment, we have only one problem to be concerned with: How we're going to get out of here. Any thinking we do has to be about that. We do not have time for side trips."

Wheeler's gray eyes remained steady. He drew a breath and looked as if he were about to say something. But he released the breath slowly and remained silent.

Around them the sand burned molten red.

Inside the pod, Vito Cracchiolo removed another piece of the control assembly and handed it out to Stone. He heard the mumble of voices from the others outside, and when McElroy's rose in anger, he was glad to be inside the pod instead of out there. Cracchiolo liked it when everything went smoothly; he did not like loud confrontations where everyone got heated up and said crazy things to each other.

So he tried to ignore the voices and concentrated on his work. His hands sorted deftly through the tangle of wires that led from the console to *jack-a-dandy*'s various control functions. Someone had made a mess of it during an earlier repair job, someone in a hurry who had not bothered to tie back the retaining harnesses in the way of a good mechanic. If Cracchiolo ever harbored a malicious thought for another human being, it was for mechanics who did not take the time to be *good* mechanics. But now he didn't mind. He could sort it out.

It was funny how something could come back to you so quickly. It had been four years since he had even looked inside the control system of a pod. But it all came back, fresh as the last time he'd assembled one there in *Hamada*'s service shop. Four years, and it was still there inside him, all the intricate wiring patterns and control components. He remembered exactly. His hands remembered, too. They knew how to work in a tight space, how to break loose a corroded bolt, how to exert just the right amount of tension without breaking something—all the tricks that came from years of experience. It felt good to get back into it, to let the hands follow remembered ways, to let the eyes and fingertips feed familiar signals to the brain—yes, it was good letting it all come back. For a moment he wanted it again.

He chuckled quietly to himself. Whistling up a dead tree, that was.

A facing plate came free, and he handed it out to Stone. A dead tree because he could not be a service mech all his life—not if he wanted to have any kind of life with Dianna and little Sam. Service mechs were long-termers—five-year minimum contracts—and a service mech's experience was good for only one thing: working on UNSA pods. Not so good being stuck for a five-year stretch on an UNSA sector ship with your family on a planet halfway across Omega.

He blinked away an eyeful of sweat and eased loose a row of connecting clips to remove another snarl of wires. He was close to the spud now; another few minutes and he would have it out. Not that he had much hope of fixing it; a spud did not lend itself to backroom repairs. But you could never tell. Maybe McElroy was right, maybe the problem was nothing more than a bad connection. Maybe. And maybe, Cracchiolo told himself with a grin, Mordinian swamphogs can fly.

The last tangle of wires came free. Behind it lay the spud, a black egg nestled up under the console shelf. The harnesses attached to the spud's housing were tight, as he had expected. Humming under his breath, he began disconnecting them.

Yes, he liked this work. Vito Cracchiolo was not such a complicated man that he had to try to convince himself otherwise. But he was also a person who was clear on his options, and he knew that Deep Space was not the place for him. Not since Dianna and little Sam had come along. The Audit Agency was his ticket home. His training at the UNSA academy on Brent, and his four-year term as staff assistant with the Audit Agency, would give him what he needed to make a living on the outside—a marketable skill in the intricate ways of UNSA accounting.

"Aren't you done yet?" grumbled Stone.

"Patience, Brother Thomas."

UNSA had its own peculiar system of accounting. It was a system designed from necessity, custom-fit around UNSA's vast array of operations. Ledger paks and operation reports were UNSA's administrative eyes and ears, its control system that kept track of the ins and outs of funds flow, of the costs and benefits, of all those quantifiable facts that kept a huge machine like UNSA from gobbling itself up with overruns and inefficiencies. Cracchiolo's homeworld of Brent had hundreds of private firms that dealt with UNSA in one way or another—and they all needed people who could understand the UNSA brand of accounting. With the training he was receiving with the Audit Agency, he was sure to get a number of offers when his name appeared on the availability roster. Offers on Brent. With his family.

Three more months.

Yes, Crackers felt good. Even the oppressive heat inside the pod did not lower his spirits. Just being alive felt good—alive with three months to go.

The last clip came loose. He handed his tools out to Stone and slipped the spud out of its housing. Stone stared at him bleakly as he shimmied out of the workspace and got to his feet. "Think you can fix it?"

Cracchiolo probed the spud's connecting pegs with a grimy fingernail. He shrugged his shoulders, but offered no answer.

It was the heat, McElroy decided, that had made him fly off the handle at Wheeler. What Wheeler had done was stupid, even dangerous. But yelling at him as if he were a child could not undo it. McElroy realized now that by venting his frustration on Wheeler he had succeeded only in aggravating an already tense situation. Which was why everyone was standing around in awkward silence when Cracchiolo came out of the pod and jumped lightly down from the rock ledge.

"We got her out, cap'n." Cracchiolo's hands and face

were smeared with greasy sweat. He handed the spud to McElroy. "Not much help, though. Can't find anything wrong with it myself."

"That's dandy," Vikki said under her breath.

McElroy looked the spud over closely. "The connections were all tight?"

"Yep. No problem there. If the trouble's with the spud, it's inside. And we're not gonna be fixing it with screwdrivers and box wrenches."

Tom Stone eased himself down backwards over the ledge, cursing as his bare hands came into contact with hot rock. He grunted something to the others and collapsed on the cargo mat.

"Is there any chance," McElroy asked without real hope, "the problem's somewhere else?"

Cracchiolo shrugged, looking doubtful. "Could be a break in the connecting circuitry. But I'll tell you, cap'n, that's not too likely. All three circuits would have to break at the same time."

"How long will it take to check them?"

Cracchiolo considered. "An hour. Maybe less."

"Oh, great," Stone grunted. He lay flat on his back on the mat, breathing heavily. "More cooked Stone, coming right up."

Cracchiolo grinned. "Stay put, Brother Thomas. From here on, it's a one-man job." He hoisted himself effortlessly to the top of the ledge and disappeared into the pod.

McElroy looked again at the spud, turning it slowly in his hand. Such a small thing to be causing so many problems. But that's the way it went—the chain's weakest link, and so forth. He placed the spud beside him on the mat, leaned back against the rock, and took his mind away to dimly remembered cool hills and blue waters.

CHAPTER TEN

McElroy came awake and sat upright, startled, then leaned slowly back against the rock. He'd been dozing for only a few minutes. Nothing had changed. The sun burned down, setting the red desert afire under a shimmering haze. Far out across the valley the malevolent trees hunched under the blazing sun, soaking up its heat and turning it dark. The distant hills flowed in shades of red and brown. The wind had died down to a searing breeze.

The four of them sought fragile shelter against the stone.

"I am going to die," Vikki Redford said disconsolately, "if I have to spend another five minutes out here."

Nobody answered her. Nobody pointed out that there was nowhere else to go but inside the pod, and that it was worse in there.

McElroy regarded the listless group through half-closed eyes. Stone was stretched out on the cargo mat, eyes shut; Redford slumped miserably beside him, looking down at her clasped hands. Only Wheeler, leaning back against the rock beside him and looking toward the distant forest, seemed to have any life left in him. McElroy realized suddenly that they could not last long in this place. If Cracchiolo were unable to get the drive system fixed, if nobody came from *Graywand* soon—if they were truly stranded here, the place would kill them, and not take long doing it.

He closed his eyes against the glare. Thinking about it would do no good.

"It wasn't always like this," Wheeler said quietly. "The desert, I mean. Geologically, it's fairly recent."

"Right," Vikki muttered without interest. McElroy kept silent. The heat was easier to bear with his eyes closed.

"They're all dead," Wheeler went on, his voice distant, mingling with the heat. "They built the city, then they died."

After a moment Vikki said, "You sound as if you blame them for it."

Wheeler made no reply, for which McElroy was grateful. It was beginning to require too much effort to listen. Too much even to think. Better to sit here and let thoughts of cool ponds and frosted glasses of brandewine flow through his brain. Better to keep the eyes shut and think of anything but the heat sizzling out there on the red sand, settling down into his bones.

"I blame them," Wheeler said suddenly. "They built a beautiful city. They shouldn't have left it. It's all falling to pieces, and it's their fault."

Vikki snorted derisively. "Come on, Wheeler. They probably died of heat prostration. You make everything so complicated."

"And you see it all so clearly." Wheeler's voice had taken on an edge. "You look at a thing, and you understand. Is that the way it is with you, Vikki?"

McElroy opened his eyes. Vikki was staring open-mouthed at Wheeler, rendered silent by his unexpected retort.

"If that's the way it is, I pity you," Wheeler went on. Even Stone sat up and squinted across at him. "If everything is so clear, so unerringly constant, if you see no mysteries, then you are not alive, and I pity you."

"John," McElroy began, "you—"

"They're dead, too." Wheeler looked again toward the forest. "Dead. And they left their city here to fall into ruin." He straightened up with a sudden laugh. It was a high, strained sound. He came to his feet quickly, like an athlete, and glared out toward the forest and the city beyond. "*Bastards!*" he shouted. "Was it worth it? Was death so divine a gift that it was worth giving up your city?"

McElroy pushed himself to his feet and stepped toward Wheeler. "Calm down, John."

Wheeler danced away, boots crackling on the hard sand. "You're all the same. You go through life with blinders on, oblivious to reality, focusing out what you don't want to see, refusing to study anything of real value. Everything's so easy that way, so simple." He spun around and shouted at the distant city. "Enjoying your immortality? *Was it worth it!?*"

"John—

He shouted at the city, cursing it in a high, strident voice as he lurched away across the sand. Stone was on his feet now, suddenly alert. He caught McElroy's eye and raised his eyebrows questioningly. McElroy made a slight, negative gesture.

Wheeler spun around. "You're all fools!" he shouted. "No better than the ones that built the city and left it to die out here. No better than all the silly fools that go through life and never see a thing outside their own petty spheres of existence. *I do not wear blinders.* I've seen something, and I will not allow you to take it away from me."

"What have you seen?" McElroy asked quietly. Wheeler was near the brink. McElroy had to somehow calm him down. "Something here? Something the rest of us missed?"

Wheeler stared at him, eyes blinking rapidly, mouth working. Then he threw back his head and laughed. "You think I'm crazy. But that doesn't matter. You're all fools. You can't understand, and I won't waste my time trying to tell you.''

Inside the pod, Cracchiolo found and repaired the connection that had burned out when the commbox overloaded. Then, humming softly to himself, he removed the bolts that held the primary drive circuit in place and unfastened the retaining clips. Starting at the point of connection to the spud's housing, he brushed away the clinging globs of corrosion and began feeling his way up the cable toward the connection at the control pad. He closed his eyes and put all his concentration into his fingertips, feeling for any variation that might indicate a break in the cable. He didn't expect to find one; cables did not break all by themselves. But his search was nonetheless thorough for the simple reason that Crackers believed in always doing things the way they should be done. He reached the cable's upper connection at the control pad, and the humming came to an abrupt stop.

The connection was—*wet*?

He brought his hand out and sniffed. Cold jo. He remembered McElroy's cup spilling when the stabilizer collapsed. *Jack-a-dandy* was an old pod. The seal around the control pad was no doubt old and cracked, and McElroy's cup of jo ran straight through and shorted out the primary circuit.

Maybe. But there were two backup circuits to take over in the event of failure in the primary circuit. He began the tracing process again, this time through the secondary circuit.

The backup circuits followed different routes between the spud and the control pad. This was by design; otherwise an accident like McElroy's cup of spilled jo would short out all three circuits at the same time. When he cleared the way to the secondary circuit after half an hour of patient manipulation, he felt his way along the cable to the control pad—and found a mass of melted insulation that could mean only one thing: the secondary circuit had overloaded.

He lay still for a moment, thinking it through. He was slimy with sweat, covered with grease and dirt and flakes of greenish-white corrosion from the control system, but he was oblivious to all this. Why had the secondary circuit failed?

He shook his head and went back to work. Get the facts. As Ma used to say, "Don't try to bake a cake without all the ingredients."

Another half hour was spent clearing the way of the tertiary circuit. Then he began the trace again. Halfway up the cable his hand encountered something that did not belong there: another cable.

Although Cracchiolo had never met Gordie Turner, it took him less than a minute to figure out what Gordie had done to the control system nearly five years earlier in *Graywand*'s service shop. The cable running from the harness to the monitor board was not, he realized immediately, a repair at all for the circuit that had obviously burned out some time ago. Rather, it was only a stopgap, put there to fool *jack-a-dandy*'s control system into thinking it had been fixed. Pretty good, Crackers thought with a trace of admiration. All this time old *jack* believed all his circuits were in working order, never suspecting that the third backup was washed out. When McElroy's jo took out the primary circuit, all the juice was diverted to the backup system. But the backup system had only half the strength it should have had. It couldn't take the surge. Poof.

Cracchiolo grinned. So simple. There was nothing at all wrong with the spud. All this time it had been nothing but a single strand of wire causing all the problems. And if he couldn't rig up a makeshift circuit in less than twenty minutes—well, if he couldn't do a simple thing like that, he would just have to admit that he'd lost his touch after all.

It required, in fact, less than ten minutes to remove the primary and secondary circuits and splice the cable connection from the spud side of the secondary to the ruined control side of the primary. He plugged his new circuit into the spud's housing and scooted out of the workspace.

That's when all the shouting began outside.

"Bastards!" Wheeler screamed at the city. He spun back around to McElroy and the others, nearly losing his footing. "Stay away from me."

Just what we need, McElroy told himself. He shook his head at Stone, who had been angling toward Wheeler from the side. He did not want to put Wheeler into a worse panic than he was in already. "What is it, John? Just tell me what—"

Again came the high, strained laughter. "Why should I tell you *anything?* You're all fools. You only see what you want to see. You can't understand real values. You won't know anything you can't *see.*"

"Sure we can. We—"

"You *can't.*" The words were spat from some inner rage. "You think I'm c-crazy, and m-maybe I am, but at least I can *see.*" He turned back toward the city with a strangled sob. "I can see what they did. I can see how they ran away from themselves and *I won't do it.*" He stumbled away across the crackling sand.

"John," McElroy called. "Wait a minute—"

Wheeler broke into a run. McElroy muttered an oath as he and Stone took out after him.

For his age, Wheeler was surprisingly agile. He ran with leg-pumping speed, dodging scrubby growths and jagged outcroppings of rock, leaping over the wide gully with ease. He ran toward the forest with single-minded determination, not once turning to look back at his pursuers.

"John!" McElroy shouted, but the hot wind took the word and cast it away. Stone, far behind, clumped to a stop after thirty yards. But McElroy had a twenty-year advantage over Wheeler and, as much damage as the heat was inflicting on him, it had to be taking an even greater toll on Wheeler. With luck, McElroy thought, he would catch Wheeler before he reached the forest.

Then McElroy stepped wrong on a jutting rock and went down, slammed into the hard-baked sand, and tumbled through a patch of scrubby vegetation that tore at his legs. He scrambled to his feet with a stream of invectives, pain lancing up through his leg as Wheeler disappeared into the first line of trees.

Stone came up, red-faced and panting. "I'll go after him—"

"Forget it," McElroy snapped. "He wants to be with his city, let him."

"We can't—"

"Yes, we can. For now, at least." McElroy tentatively placed weight on his ankle, and winced. All he needed to top off the day was a sprained ankle. "Let's get back to the pod."

They would have to go after Wheeler, McElroy told himself as he hobbled toward *jack-a-dandy* with Stone's help. They couldn't let him wander about in that desert alone. But they would do it the right way, not go off half-cocked, and get lost out there with the blistering heat waiting to cook them alive at the first opportunity. No more mistakes. There had been more than enough already.

Cracchiolo was standing beside Vikki Redford when they reached the ledge. McElroy waved away his offer to help and eased himself down onto the cargo mat, still fuming inwardly at Wheeler. "What are you doing out here? You get the drive system fixed?"

"Sure," Cracchiolo said nonchalantly. "Nothing to it."

Three sets of eyes turned to Cracchiolo and widened.

"You fixed the drive?" Vikki asked incredulously. "You really did it?"

"Yeah, really." Cracchiolo grinned broadly. "The cap'n was right. The circuitry shorted out. Didn't really take much to make up a new set."

"We can get out of here?"

Cracchiolo nodded. "All we have to do is plug in the spud."

"And," Stone added, "track Wheeler down. We can't very well leave without him."

A brief silence was broken by McElroy. "Some of us can." He turned to Cracchiolo. "You and Vikki skip to *Graywand* and send back the Blue. We'll let them do the looking for Wheeler."

Cracchiolo frowned. "You and Brother Thomas staying here?"

"That's right."

The frown deepened. "I don't know, cap'n—"

"How long will it take you to get the pod ready to go?"

Cracchiolo shrugged. "A few minutes to tie up the loose ends, that's all."

"Then you can get to *Graywand* and be back here with help in less than an hour. That makes a lot more sense than all of us tramping around in the desert without the right equipment."

"We have emergency lifesuits and sounders."

"But we don't have the experience," McElroy said. "The risk is too great."

"He's right," Stone said. "Let the Blue do it. They'll have a better chance than we will of finding John."

Cracchiolo stood for a moment longer, not comfortable with the idea of leaving McElroy and the others here. But he gave in at last with a slight movement of his shoulders. "You're the boss, cap'n. You got the spud?"

McElroy was straightening out his leg, trying to ease some of the throbbing pain. "What?"

"The spud. I left it out here. Where is it?"

It was gone. They spent several minutes searching before they believed it.

"It was right here," Vikki said, lifting the end of the cargo mat to look under it for the third time. "It couldn't have gotten up and walked away."

"You're right," McElroy agreed. "So what happened to it?"

"Wheeler took it." Stone's calm statement jolted through the gathering panic. "I saw him fooling around with it. I never thought he'd take it."

"Why would he do a crazy thing like that?" McElroy demanded, swinging around to face Stone. "Why take the spud, of all things?"

Stone shrugged his heavy shoulders. "Maybe he doesn't want us to leave just yet."

McElroy shook his head in exasperation. The state Wheeler was in, anything was possible. "We don't have any choice, then. We'll have to go after him."

CHAPTER ELEVEN

Vikki Redford and Tom Stone made their way along the edge of a deep gully, the sand crackling under their boots, the hot wind at their backs. The massive ruin seemed to take on a hunched, menacing look as they neared it. Vikki could only vaguely discern the pentagonal shape Wheeler had described; a tomb, he had called it, and it was easy enough to believe that somehow he was right. It squatted there among the stunted trees, and she could not shake the feeling that it was watching her. She had to remind herself that it was only a pile of stone.

It was certain that Wheeler had gone into the structure. Cracchiolo had attuned wrist sounders for Vikki and Stone to match the one worn by Wheeler, and he'd instructed them on how to read the colors and patterns of the lighted dials. The sounders led without question to this hulking structure. Whatever the reasons Wheeler's sun-baked brain had provided, this was where he'd gone.

Vikki stopped to mop the sweat from her brow. It would

be cooler inside all that rock. If they accomplished nothing else, at least they would be able to get out of the hot sun for a while. She glanced up at the massive ruin, then looked away quickly to scan the distant forest. "Any idea how we're going to get inside?"

No response. She turned and saw Stone twenty paces back, prodding at something with the toe of his boot. "*Stone!*"

He looked up, startled by her shout. "Sorry. Tripped over something and stopped to look."

"Yeah, well, lift your feet from now on."

"Sure."

She waited for him to catch up and move past, then followed silently, irritated by his seeming lack of concern; in a few minutes they would have to go inside that hulking edifice and look for Wheeler.

Hulking edifice. There I go again, she thought.

Not that she was frightened by the prospect. Well, maybe a little, but certainly not as much as she'd expected to be. Halfway through the ruined city, with the stone structure seeming to take on new proportions with each step, she regretted her big-mouthed insistence on coming out here. But really, when it came down to it, she'd had no choice. McElroy couldn't make the trip, not with an ankle that had taken on the dimensions of a grapefruit. Crackers had to put the drive system back together, which left Vikki and Tom to track Wheeler down and bring him, and the spud, back.

But the trek had become less than appealing even before they left the pod. For one thing, McElroy was adamant in his insistence that they wear the lifesuits Crackers found in *jack-a-dandy*'s emergency store. The lifesuits—single-piece, tight-fitting coveralls designed to insulate the body from extremes of temperature—would protect them from dehydration. Which, Vikki admitted, was a decent reason for wearing them. But she had never liked lifesuits and in fact had not worn one in years. They clung to the skin; in Vikki's mind, only replacing one discomfort with another. To get it on she'd had to strip down naked in front of three men, all of whom were lecherous enough to watch from the corners of their eyes while pretending to do other things. Then one of the flexos jammed as she was unrolling the suit over herself, and after struggling for a few minutes with her bare breasts hanging out, she was forced to ask McElroy for help.

All things considered, not a propitious start. And now that they were here, the prospect of going inside that mound of rock somehow had even less appeal than she'd expected it to have. Not that she was afraid.

They were close to the base of the ruin now, stepping carefully over rubble that had fallen from the sloping sides. Not exactly what she'd planned to be doing as staff auditor on *Graywand*. She was an accountant, not a Blue. Not yet, at least. She had no business tramping around in a place like this, running the risk of being stranded on this hellhole ball of sand. Not on an accountant's salary. A typical screwup. UNSA was so overloaded with incompetents—

"There's an opening up ahead."

Stone's words startled her. She jerked around, then clamped down on her jittery nerves and followed his pointing finger. Ahead of them she saw a jagged fissure in the stone wall of the structure, formed when one massive slab of rock had pulled free of the others and split open.

"Forget it," she said. "We couldn't fit in there."

"It wouldn't hurt to take a look."

"How do you know it wouldn't hurt?" She looked at the narrow fracture. Stone was crazy if he thought she was going to get down on her hands and knees and crawl into that black hole. "It might hurt plenty if there's something waiting in there for us."

"I'll bet that's where Wheeler went in." Then, after a short pause, "Anyway, we have our sizzlers."

"We'll find another way in."

"Yeah, but we might miss him. Even if we find another way inside, we might have to backtrack all the way through to find him."

He was right. She knew that, but she stood in stormy silence, trying to conjure up one solid reason for not going in through that fracture, wondering at the same time why she was so loath to do it. She had no fear of caves. A long time ago, maybe—just a touch of claustrophobia in close places. But she'd outgrown that. And anyway, she and Stone carried powerful lanterns on their belts, so it wouldn't be dark inside. Chances were good the fracture didn't even penetrate through to the inside. It probably went in only a few meters. They wouldn't have to go far to see that, and it would satisfy Stone.

"All right," she said at last. "Let's take a look."

A brief look of relief crossed Stone's face.

"You don't have to be so smug about it," she snapped.

"What?"

"Oh, never mind."

With a slight shrug of incomprehension, Stone stepped over a pile of debris and squatted at the crumbled wall. He unclipped the lantern from his belt and shifted forward onto the balls of his feet, holding the overhanging lip of rock with one hand as he flashed the beam far back into the fracture. "Looks like it goes back a good ways. Let's take a look."

There was nothing for it. She had come this far, and she could not turn back now.

Getting in through the narrow opening was bad, but it was not the worst part. The fracture was even more constricted inside than she had thought. They were forced to hunch along slowly, packs scraping the jagged stones above while hands and knees stirred up choking dust. Vikki kept silent, grim in her determination to let Stone find his dead end so they could turn around and get out of here.

But the fracture twisted and turned its way far back into the rock, never quite coming to an end. They had been worming their way into it for a quarter of an hour before they reached a place where they could stand. The fracture widened here where one massive boulder, under thousands of tons of stress, had shattered, leaving a good part of itself on the sloping floor but opening up just enough room for her and Stone to stand close together with Stone's head brushing the ceiling. They studied the small cavern with lights set on low beam and wide angle. It felt good to stand, to get the cricks out. It was almost cool in here, out of the blazing sun.

But standing there, listening to their breathing in the cramped space, feeling awkward so close to the sweating Stone, Vikki could not help being aware of the tremendous weight around them, of all that rock piled on their heads. All those tons of rock, pressing down, pressing—

She remembered with chilling clarity her earlier self-assurance about having outgrown her childhood fear of the dark.

"Tom." She spoke the word softly, keeping her brittle nerves under control by an effort of will.

"Hmmm?" He was working with his lantern, suddenly interested in an opening he'd found beside the jutting edge of a huge stone.

Vikki drew a breath. There was no reason to feel this way. No reason at all, but she did, and that was reality for you. Even if it made no sense, it was there, along with all those tons of rock pressing down. She bit down hard on her lower lip and tried to think of something else.

"Wheeler went through here." Stone tested the rubble just below the jutting corner, prodding at the hole with a gloved hand. "We'll have to widen it to get my fat rump through. Hold the light, will you?"

Feeling slightly disjointed, she watched as Stone began digging with both hands, scooping up loose rock, working out fist-sized pieces and tossing them against the opposite wall. The tiny cavern filled with a suffocating haze of dust.

"Almost through," he said. She stood behind him, trying to cope with the surrealistic aspect the scene had taken on. She gripped the light in a rigid fist. Her throat was closed up tight, as if the floating mist of dust had congealed the tissues, laid thick fingers over her vocal chords to silence them. Crazy, crazy, crazy to be so afraid of this place. She watched Stone working at the wall and felt as if she'd spent an eternity entombed in this vault.

"No reason to worry about bringing the roof down on us," he said conversationally as he eased out a head-sized rock and rolled it away. "It's been here a long time. Chances are it'll last another few hours." Another boulder tumbled across the floor. "That's got it. Let's go." He began climbing through the opening.

CHAPTER TWELVE

Oliver McElroy shielded his eyes against the glare and looked out across the simmering desert. Vikki and Tom had been gone little more than an hour. There was no reason to expect them back so soon, but he looked nonetheless, simply because he had nothing better to do.

A month's pay, he decided. That was how much he would have given at that moment for a cold drink. Ice? Throw in another month.

"Uh, cap'n? We got a problem here." Cracchiolo stood in the open hatchway of the pod, looking down at him. His face was strangely pale. "The console's lit up like a Christmas tree."

Now what? McElroy asked himself. Gritting his teeth at the pain it brought to his swollen ankle, he climbed up to the pod, ducked through the hatchway, and lowered himself wearily into the control chair. Two of the lights in the row of green above the readout screen had changed to red. A message flashed across the screen:

WARNING WARNING WARNING
DRIVE ENGINE MALFUNCTION

. . .

WARNING WARNING WARNING
DRIVE ENGINE MALFUNCTION

. . .

WARNING WARNING WARNING
DRIVE ENGINE MALFUNCTION

"This is big trouble, cap'n." Cracchiolo stood beside him, staring fixedly at the screen. "The engines are heating up."

WARNING WARNING WARNING

McElroy turned to look up at Cracchiolo. "They're not even activated. How can they be heating up?"

Cracchiolo shook his head. "Not from high temperature. Energy buildup. Imbalances inside the engines. Instability because the spud isn't controlling them anymore."

WARNING WARNING WARNING
DRIVE ENGINE MALFUNCTION

A gust of wind rattled sand against the outside of the pod. *This must be very bad*, McElroy thought, *if it's got Crackers upset.*

"I heard about something like this once," Cracchiolo went on. "It happened on a planet called Osiris. Somewhere in the upper part of the Hyades, I think." He licked his lips, watching the readout screen. "Long time ago, before they built in the fail-safe between the spud and the engines. Just one of those things. One in a million, everyone said. Connecting circuit between the spud and the drive engines went out." Pause. "You want some jo, cap'n?"

"No," McElroy answered tersely. "What happened?"

"The engines blew. There's something—I don't know exactly—some kind of permanent balance that keeps the field where it belongs." He looked directly at McElroy for the first time. "That's all the spud does, you know. Keeps the field in its place. The field's always there, somewhere in the link between the spud and the engines. Balance gets screwed up if the link's busted. That's what happened on Osiris. Engine couldn't take the strain. Wiped out about a thousand square kilometers of the planet, as I recall."

McElroy stared at Cracchiolo a moment longer, then turned to the console and hit the break key with more force than was necessary.

EXPLAIN LAST MESSAGE

Jack-a-dandy responded:

DRIVE ENGINE MALFUNCTION
READY:

McElroy chewed his lower lip. Cracchiolo kept silent behind him. The pod shuddered under another gust of wind. Then McElroy keyed a single word into the control pad:

MORE

To this, *jack-a-dandy* responded promptly:

DUE TO MALFUNCTION IN R-WAVE RELAY SYSTEM
OF KOHLMANN STREAM COMMUTATOR
DISEQUILIBRIUM OF ENGINE SYSTEM MR-40
RIGHT QUADRANT WAVE STABILIZATION
WILL RESULT IN
KOHLMANN STREAM MR-40 EQUALIZATION AT
08:15:27GC
OR
FORCED EQUILIBRIUM OF ENGINE SYSTEM MR-40

```
RIGHT QUADRANT WAVE
STABILIZATION AT
10:53:05
READY . . .
```

The message was squeezed together so it would all fit on the screen at the same time. McElroy read through it twice. "Any idea what that means?"

"Yeah, cap'n, I got an idea. It means we have to get the spud hooked into the drive system within the next eight hours and fifteen minutes. That's the point of no return. After that it will be too late."

"Too late?" Despite the heat, McElroy felt a chill along his spine.

Cracchiolo nodded. "Two and a half hours later the drive engines will blow a crater in this planet big enough to bury a sector ship in. And we won't be able to do a thing about it."

Vicki would never have believed that anything Stone could do or say would make her squirm through that hole in the crumbling wall. But the simple fact was that she could not stay inside the stifling, dust-filled cavern a moment longer. When faced with the choice of escaping through Stone's gouged-out hole or slithering alone back through the crack to the outside, there was really no choice at all. So she followed him through to the inside.

And they *were* inside. Vikki had hoped—had almost built up a certainty in her mind—that they would discover that this great mound of rock was, after all, nothing more than that. A monument, perhaps, like the old pyramids of ancient Terra. But her hopes died when they crawled through the opening and came out into a dusty corridor that stretched out away from them in both directions. It was narrow, barely wide enough for the two of them to stand side by side, with a ceiling so low that even Vikki was forced to stoop. Her claustrophobia was still there, just below the surface, but it was made tolerable by something that was infinitely worse: an overpowering stench—

death and decay, conjuring up visions of slimy things that grew in moist soil. She had to swallow to keep from gagging.

"This's really something."

She turned to stare at Stone where he hunched beside her under the low ceiling, looking around with wide eyes, face underlit by the backwash of light from their lanterns. "Wheeler was right. There's something special about this place. It's—"

"It's something special, all right," she interrupted. "Can't you smell it?" Then she was sorry she'd raised her voice, because the walls picked up the sound and bounced it all around and sent a chill rippling along her spine. The odor of death seemed to be getting stronger, carried on warm currents of air. She tensed, rocking forward on the balls of her feet.

"Looks like we're on his track."

She jumped and spun around angrily. *"Will you stop that!"*

Stone gave her an odd look. "All I meant was, the sounder's picked up Wheeler." He looked ridiculous hunched under the ceiling like a giant toad, peering down at the instrument on his wrist. The colored lines had gone wavy. "Let's go this way." He began moving down the corridor. After a quick sweep of her light, Vikki steadied her nerves and followed.

The corridor bore straight away from them, stone-gray in the twin beams of light, fading out to black far ahead. A thick layer of dust covered everything, rose up around their boots and fogged the air, sticking to the exposed skin of their necks and faces. Vikki had never been so sick of dust and grit in her life. She followed behind Stone, bent over, feeling the walls close on either side. Their lanterns pierced the swirling dust to show the way, but the narrow beams were thin and cold, providing little comfort.

There was nothing here to be afraid of. Nothing in here but harmless old Wheeler and his crazy ideas. And the spud. Nothing to be afraid of. She told herself that over and over, but the fears came anyway, creeping up through her stomach to make the flesh of her arms feel cold and prickly under the lifesuit. Silly, she told herself, trying to smile at her foolishness. There was nothing here to be afraid of, nothing to give her that feeling inside, a feeling like something was watching her, a feeling almost like some horrible, slimy thing was creeping around inside her—

She stumbled as a breath of putrid air brushed across her face. It was worse than anything she'd ever experienced, worse even than the time an old seabuck beached itself a half mile from her home on Zarifa. She was ten then, with a youngster's fascination with death. Three days after the giant had come ashore, just before it was trucked away by men who wore masks over their faces and cursed loudly, she snuck down for a final look. The seabuck was plenty ripe by then—she lost her breakfast that morning to the white sand—but the stench of that bloated carcass was as nothing to the putrid smell of decay that hit her now.

She made a sound and Stone, who had moved on ahead, turned in surprise. "You okay?"

She gagged, thought she was going to be sick, belched, and knew she had forestalled it for another few seconds. "Can't you smell that—that—" She had to stop to swallow the bile that was rising in her throat. He could not be that oblivious to the suffocating stench.

Stone lifted his nose and sniffed. "It does smell a bit rank in here." He flashed his light around, then pointed toward a crack running between the wall and the floor. "It's coming from down there. Smells like something died."

She stared at him incredulously, thinking that he had the most amazing gift for understatement she had ever encountered.

He turned to go on, then stopped suddenly as something caught his attention. He peered at the wall, holding his light so the beam fell obliquely across the gray surface.

''There's something strange here.'' He bent for a closer look, probing with a fingernail. ''Hmmm.''

Then Vikki saw it: a tiny crack—too straight to be a stress fault—running up the wall nearly covered with dust. It angled across and—it wasn't a crack at all but a door, fitted so tightly into the wall that they could easily have gone right past without seeing it.

Then Stone moved his light, and she saw the faint outlines of many doors along the corridor. They became visible in a rush, as if seeing one had attuned her eyes to all the rest. They were small, less than a meter square; three tiers of them stretching along the wall as far as she could see, separated by narrow strips of gray wall. Like a massive cupboard, she thought, a cupboard with hundreds of doors and no handles. Stone swung his light across to the other side of the corridor, and the doors were there, too, as Vikki had known they would be.

''The entire structure is like this, I'll bet,'' he said wonderingly.

Yes, she thought. *Corridor after corridor of little safe-deposit boxes.*

''It's a vault,'' Stone said. ''I wonder what's behind all these doors. Could be the biggest find in this part of Omega.''

''The Blue,'' she broke in loudly. ''That's who it's for. Now let's get moving. What are you doing?''

Stone pulled a small prybar from a compartment of his belt pack and went to work on the nearest door, coaxing the tool's flat edge into the crack between the door and the wall. ''Doubt if we can get it open,'' he said. ''But it can't hurt to give it a try.''

''Can't hurt—?'' She stared at him stupidly. ''Stone, you cannot open that door.''

''You're probably right,'' he agreed, working with the bar.

She watched for a moment, unable to speak. Pieces of rock flaked away as the crack widened. She could think of all sorts of ways it could hurt. The whole place could be an elaborate booby trap, waiting for someone with fatal curiosity to blunder along and set it off. Or, God help them, what if there were something alive in there? Not possible, reported her logic centers, but they were shouted down by other parts of her brain, those parts which had come to believe that anything was possible in this place.

Just as the words found themselves and she opened her mouth to tell Stone to get away from that wall—stepped forward to forcibly pull him away if necessary—something rattled behind the door, and it creaked open. Stone stepped back as it thudded solidly against the wall and shattered, as if made of brittle porcelain.

Behind the door was a shallow vault. Vikki looked at the thing that lay waiting inside and took an involuntary step back. Then she began screaming.

CHAPTER THIRTEEN

Graywand's operations library was a small fourth-level room situated almost as an afterthought between the main recreation lounge and the officers' mess. It had few visitors. The operations personnel who made use of its records did so via terminal access at their own posts. The library was sparsely furnished with a half dozen viewscreens arranged along one stark gray wall, a large file cabinet with indexed drawers built into the opposite, equally unadorned wall, and a cluttered woodtone desk behind which sat a gaunt, hard-eyed librarian who was not about to let the junior clerk from CommSec use one of her screens without the proper authorization.

"You'll need Mr. Spick's approval on the prescribed form before you can see the files," she repeated curtly. "There are no exceptions."

"I'm sure the information I want isn't classified."

"Everything is classified, young man," she retorted. "The question is merely one of degree. If you were entitled to general library access, you would undoubtedly possess your own terminal and authorization codes. The fact that you have neither indicates to me that you are not entitled to general access."

"I'm in CommSec. That gives me four-zero clearance."

"Good. You should have no problem securing access authorization from Mr. Spick. If you'll excuse me, I'm behind as it is." She returned to her papers.

It had not occurred to Lars that he might have trouble getting into the library's file on Sierra. The post was a well-established commercial enterprise; there was nothing secret about it. "I'm sorry to be a bother," he persisted, "but you see, I—"

"No," she snapped, scribbling furiously, her head down.

Lars knew that Raymond Spick would never give his approval once he found out why Lars wanted the Sierra file. The CommSec Director had made quite clear his insistence that no department outside CommSec be brought into the picture.

"Ma'am?"

The librarian's head snapped up. She slammed her pencil down and leaned back in her chair, glaring up at Lars. "You are persistent, Mr. Clemens. That is ordinarily a trait I admire. But you do not listen very well. I will try to speak clearly this time: Until Mr. Spick gives his permission, you will not be allowed to view the Sierra file, or any other file in my library. I cannot make myself more explicit than that."

"I understand, ma'am. It was wrong of me to think you would overlook such an important regulation. If you have one of the authorization forms, I'll take it to Mr. Spick now for his signature."

"This is a library, not a supply room," she informed him acidly. "I do not dispense authorization forms. Now, if you will excuse me."

"Yes, ma'am," Lars said apologetically. Then: "What form was that?"

"Twenty-nine sixty-six," she spat out, reaching the end of her patience. "*Now,* if you'll—"

"Thank you, ma'am."

Five minutes later Lars was in the eighth-level supply cubby.

"How're you doin', Lars?"

"Fine, Herman. Listen, I'm in a big hurry. Spick's after my tail. You got some twenty-nine sixty-six in stock?"

Herman Griffin pursed his thick lips, searching through his mental catalog. Herman was manager of *Graywand*'s office services department. He was a big, good-natured man with a sloppy grin and a down-home face. "Authorization form for internal data access. Sure, I have some of those."

"Spick needs a dozen of them right away."

"You have a slip for it?"

Lars blinked. "A slip?"

"Request voucher. Spick has to sign for anything going to CommSec." Herman shrugged his heavy shoulders. "Control, you know."

It never ended. Authorization forms needed for authorization forms. "Oh, yeah. It's right here." Lars fished inside the pocket of his tunic, then put a puzzled look on his face and made a show of feeling in each of his other pockets. "Darn. It was right here."

"Sorry, Lars. I can't let you have the forms without a voucher," Herman said apologetically. "Tell you what I'll do. I'll give Spick a call and ask him to give his okay verbally."

"Well—" Lars hesitated. "I don't know about that, Herman. I'm already on Spick's list. He's likely to come down hard on me if he finds out I lost his request voucher." He went through his pockets again, feeling lousy about what he was doing. "Nuts. It was right here."

"Things like that happen. Spick'll understand."

"Sure," Lars said wryly. "Do you know Raymond Spick?"

Herman thought it over. "I know what you mean." Herman was not, Lars knew, an admirer of Spick. "Ah, why not," he said at last. "Nobody'll ever know." He reached below the counter and brought up a pad of request vouchers which he placed in front of Lars. "Fill out one of these and put your own name at the bottom."

While Herman got the data authorization forms from a back room, Lars completed the voucher and scrawled a signature that he hoped was illegible. The charade had worked, but Lars did not feel proud of it. He liked Herman Griffin; he did not like lying to him. The fact that it was necessary did little to help the sick feeling it caused in the pit of his stomach.

Herman filed the voucher in a drawer under the counter, then slipped the stack of forms into a large envelope and handed it to Lars.

"Thanks, Herman. I owe you."

The big man shrugged away the debt. "Forget it, Lars. Glad I could help."

"Any luck?" Carl Lunsford asked as Lars hurried into the CommSec cubby and began looking through the cluttered drawers of his desk.

"You wouldn't believe— Ah!" Lars extracted a copy of a memorandum from Raymond Spick, a notice about a routine staff meeting that had long since come and gone, from a bottom drawer and slipped it into the envelope Herman had given him. "Has Spalding been down?"

Lunsford looked at him. "Are you serious?"

"You haven't heard from McElroy, I suppose?"

Lunsford shook his head. "Afraid not."

Lars turned to go, the envelope tucked under his arm. "I'll be in the library."

"Take care, Lars. You're treading dangerous waters."

Clutching the bulky envelope under his arm, Lars took an elevator to the fourth level and went into one of the curtained game alcoves in the recreation lounge. Ignoring the flickering game screens, he opened the envelope and shook its contents out onto the small countertop used for players' drinks. He looked down at the stack of authorization forms and the memorandum from Raymond Spick.

On the sixth try, he produced what he considered to be a fair imitation of Spick's signature. It was not a good one; it would not withstand close scrutiny. But it would serve the purpose. He filled in the rest of the form, then returned the memorandum and the blank authorization forms to the envelope. In the corridor outside, he dropped the envelope into a disposal chute and two minutes later placed the completed authorization on the librarian's desk.

She looked it over with a scowl, examining every line with a deliberateness that made Lars sweat. Then she keyed a brief command into the pad at her desk and snapped, "The Sierra file is available on screen six."

Lars gave an inward sigh of relief and went to work. Two hours later he was more confused than ever.

The Sierra file was his only lead, his only chance of finding the link to the audit team's disappearance. But after reviewing every report and piece of correspondence that appeared on the screen, he found no mention whatever of an incorrect skip to Sierra, not a word about the incident Rod Clawson had told him about. As far as the Sierra file was concerned, it had never happened. He rubbed his eyes wearily and returned to the desk.

The librarian was outraged by Lars's questioning of the adequacy of her files. "Anything of importance is in there. I can assure you of that."

"Yes, ma'am." Lars gestured toward the row of indexed drawers lining the wall. "Are those library files?"

"Certainly. But there is nothing in those files that could be of interest to you. They include nothing but backup documentation for data included elsewhere. You have already seen everything of importance."

"Would there be a file in there for Sierra?"

"Yes," she snapped, her voice like a whip. She glared at him a moment longer, then rose and brushed past him, striding to a point midway down the row of files where, after a quick scan of the index numbers, she jerked open one of the drawers. After a moment's search, she extracted a bulky folder and handed it to him, accompanying the action with a harsh sound deep in her throat.

Lars took the packet to a small bench alongside the screen he'd used earlier. Inside he found a potpourri of documents ranging from equipment repair orders to supply requisitions to project status reports. Conscious of time passing, he began the wearisome chore of sorting through the file.

An hour later he found what he was looking for.

"It's an interdepartmental memo," said Carl Lunsford, frowning down at the ragged scrap of paper Lars had given him. The paper was stained with what looked to be spilled jo; one corner had been ripped away. "It was sent from one Blue to another. Where'd you find it?"

"In the Sierra file. I smuggled it out of the library."

Lunsford'd frown deepened. "This is the original copy. It should have gone to this guy Bannat."

"I know. The routing orders were torn off."

"Dumb mail clerks," Lunsford said. "If they'd just looked at it, they would've known where to send it." He looked up at Lars. "This could be serious."

"I know that." Lars took the memorandum and reread the brief message. Its meaning was clear: Jack Bannat of Field Recon had landed a new planet, a planet he called Tartarus. Later, somebody else in the Blue discovered that Bannat had inadvertently given the new planet a bad set of coordinates.

It was all spelled out in the memo. Tartarus had been given the coordinates already assigned to the planet called Sierra.

Tartarus. A new planet, not yet surveyed, with no development of any kind. And, without a doubt, that was where Oliver McElroy and his team of auditors had gone.

CHAPTER FOURTEEN

When Vikki could control herself enough to look more closely at the thing in the vault, she realized that she was looking at the remains of a living creature. It was vaguely humanoid: a fragile ribcage and pelvis ending in a spindly pair of legs; many-jointed arms with tiny hands that had several fingers—more than five, Vikki thought, although she did not count them; a small, round skull with all the important fixtures in the right places. Shreds of clothing and gray skin clung to a delicate skeletal structure that had itself begun to deteriorate around the empty eye sockets and the small bones of the hands and feet. It was laid out flat in its narrow crypt, exposed with obscene clarity in the glare of Stone's lantern.

"Wheeler was right," Stone said, his voice tinged with wonder. "The place is a tomb." The beam of his light swept back along the gray wall, past all those other sealed doors. "There must be thousands of them in here."

Vikki made a small sound. She did not want to think

about all those vaults with little bodies stretched out inside, turning to dust. It was bad enough thinking of the tomb itself, of the rock above their heads, of the dusty gray walls pressing close against their shoulders. Bad enough to think all those thoughts without adding to them death and decay, thousands of mummified bodies.

"This'll keep the arkies busy for years," Stone was saying. "And this place is *old*. It's—"

That was when Vikki heard it.

It was only a small sound, a scrabbling sound of something alive, clawed feet against a stone floor.

She spun around, knocking herself almost senseless on the low ceiling.

"What was that?" Stone asked. "Did you hear something?"

"Shut up!" she whispered fiercely. She strained to see through the blackness, the forgotten light in her clenched fist pointing at the floor.

Then it came again, closer this time. Cold horror curled thickly about her as she realized that whatever was making that scratching sound was between them and the narrow cleft in the rock, blocking the only way out. Blood thumped thickly in her ears, drowning out all reason. She gripped her sizzler in one fist and the useless light in the other. Her mouth was dry and sour.

"Must be Wheeler," Stone decided aloud. "John, is that—?"

"Will you shut up!"

More sounds of tapping and scraping came toward them from the blackness. Even Wheeler couldn't make sounds like that. No human could, because human feet were not equipped with claws.

"I think—"

"SHUT UP!"

Her scream echoed down the passageway. The sounds stopped. She waited, hardly breathing. Even Stone kept quiet.

Silence.

She ran out of air and drew a breath. More silence.

Maybe she had let the place get to her, she thought. Maybe the skittering noises were only mice.

Mice. Yes, of course. Mice. Or this planet's equivalent of mice. Little furry rodents. Tiny things with pointy ears and long tails. She and Stone had disturbed them. She almost laughed aloud. She did not blame the poor frightened things for running about.

She opened her mouth to speak, to tell Stone how stupid they'd been to be afraid of mice, when the breath caught in her throat and froze there.

Something was staring at her through the darkness.

Something with red eyes—bloated red eyes like bloody clots. She had been looking at them for a long time, not quite realizing what they were. Then they moved closer, and she knew. Something large was behind those eyes, something that lurked there on the gray floor, filling the corridor with the smell of rotting flesh. More sounds added a new dimension to the horror—wheezings and gurglings, thick, moist sounds that could not possibly come from tiny rodents.

She swung the lantern and the sizzler up at the same time, fumbled them together, and somehow dropped the lantern. It hit hard against the stone floor and went out. She pressed the sizzler's firing stud, moving the weapon from side to side, sweeping the corridor with crackling death. She knew that she was nearly paralyzed with terror. She knew also that if she did not follow through with the motion she'd started, she would collapse into a frothing heap and poor big dumb Stone would never in a million years get them out of here in one piece.

She finally released the stud and held the sizzler out in front of her. The corridor was silent. She could see nothing but dancing spots against the blackness. The blue fire had blinded her.

"Get that light up here," she whispered hoarsely. She crouched low, heart hammering in her chest, and steadied the sizzler, ready to burn to a crisp whatever was out there. She felt strangely confident now, as if she had passed the ultimate test. The worst had happened, and now she was calm. She could do whatever had to be done.

Stone brought his lantern up, beaming it past her into the corridor, flashing it from side to side against the dull gray surfaces.

The corridor was empty.

No red-eyed monsters or scampering rodents. No long-dead decaying corpses crawling out of their vaults to come after the violators of their sanctum. Nothing but dust.

She crouched motionless for a long time, listening to the silence, watching the beam play along the ancient rock, throwing shadows in a crazy dance of dark and light. She became aware that she was holding her breath. She sucked in more air, then held it again, unconsciously, waiting.

"Whatever it was," Stone said quietly, "it's gone now. Let's—"

He broke off as Vikki grasped his forearm and squeezed harshly. She did not need a Stone dissertation right now. She needed to think.

The thing with the red eyes had backed around the corner into an adjoining passageway. There was no other place for it to go. It was there, waiting for them, crouching in the silent darkness, not even breathing because it knew that sooner or later they would believe it had gone and come strolling down the corridor.

Suddenly the strain of waiting was more than she could bear. She yanked the lantern away from a startled Tom Stone and ran down the passageway to the corner, making straight for the waiting whatever-it-was. Then she was there, skidding around the corner, thrusting the sizzler out in front of her to squeeze off a barrage of pulses. Blue fire spattered against the far wall, lived a brief moment, and died. The beam of light stabbed out, darted back and forth, touching only dust and gray stone and black emptiness.

She stood breathing the scorched air. A muscle twitched in her cheek; her legs tensed, wanting to run. She moved the light from side to side, waiting for the thing with the red eyes to come at her as she stood there half-frozen. But only the dust and silence waited with her.

Then something moved behind her. She spun around, finger tightening on the firing stud of her sizzler. The lantern's powerful beam of light caught Stone full in the face. For one jittery moment she thought she would burn him were he stood, that even knowing it was Stone would not be enough to stop the flood of signals from her brain to her finger, commanding it to press the firing stud. Then, slowly, the tension eased from her finger, and she let the weapon fall to her side.

"Mind getting that light out of my eyes?" Stone asked casually.

All the muscles in her arms seemed stiff and sluggish. She drew a ragged breath. "Let's go back, Stone. Let's go back to the pod and get out of this place."

"I wish we could." Stone consulted the sounder on his wrist. "Wheeler's not too far ahead. Let's get moving."

She couldn't do it. Not ever. She was frozen here, her legs in mutiny. There was only so much a person could take before coming apart, and she had the full measure already.

But somehow, when Stone adjusted his light to wide angle and struck off down the passageway, Vikki's feet called on some inner courage and her legs abandoned their mutinous cause and carried her along behind him. She felt remote and unattached, as if someone else's body were moving through this nightmare with her along merely as an observer.

The corridor was narrow, but it was straight and clear of obstructions. Stone moved rapidly along, ignoring the intersecting passageways that branched off at regular intervals, stirring up dust and putrid air, with Vikki almost gagging in his wake. She turned constantly to sweep her light behind her at sounds that may have been only in her mind. She kept close to Stone, tripping over his heels more than once.

After what seemed like a long time, they reached the end of the corridor. It did not, as Vikki had expected, merge into another one, but ended at a vertical shaft that dropped several meters to another stone floor, where another narrow corridor stretched away into darkness.

Stone consulted the sounder. Vikki saw him frown in the backwash of light. "Wheeler's below us," he said. "He must've jumped. Looks like quite a distance to jump."

"Wheeler can do whatever he wants. Personally, I don't feel like breaking a leg—" Vikki broke off suddenly, spinning around, swinging her lantern in an arc. The rustling sounds had not been her imagination this time. She caught a glimpse of them, the light brushing them just as they disappeared into connecting corridors—gray shadows close to the ground, skittering for cover at the edge of the powerful beam. The sizzler was in her hand, waving unsteadily, trying to fix on a target as the shadows merged into darkness.

Then the full extent of their situation struck her: the shaft at their backs, red-eyed creatures filling the corridors and blocking the only way of escape.

"Tom, I can't—" she began. Then her throat closed up tight, and she could say no more. The rustling sounds quieted, to be replaced by the infinitely worse gurglings and mewlings that echoed eerily through the corridors.

Stone touched her arm. "Don't panic."

Don't panic. Stone's profound contribution. Vikki almost laughed.

"Keep me covered," he said. "I'll get the powerlift set up."

Keep me covered. She'd never heard that phrase used in real life. Stone was being quite amusing today. She frowned. "Powerlift?"

"Right. To get us down the shaft." She could hear him fumbling with his pack.

"Stone—" she began; then a sudden movement at the

fringe of light made her jerk her sizzler around. Blue flame spattered harmlessly against the wall, stirring up a wisp of gray dust. The shadow scuttled into an adjoining corridor. Whatever they were, they were fast. "Stone," she began again, keeping her eyes fixed on the corridor, "I do not want to go down that shaft."

"We have to," he said matter-of-factly. "Wheeler's down there somewhere. We can't leave him. Besides, we need the spud."

She licked dry lips and started to say something, then jerked the lantern up as another shadow moved. They were coming closer, darting from one intersecting corridor to another, always keeping just outside the beam of light. Behind her there was a brief grinding sound, followed by a solid snap. Powerlift: thirty meters of high-strength cord with a hooked fastener at one end and a power attachment at the other. The powerlift was standard equipment in every emergency pack, although Vikki hadn't used one since her course in emergency procedures at the academy. She suddenly remembered, with almost laughable clarity, the black-haired instructor of that long-ago course. He had had the most beautiful brown eyes Vikki had ever seen. She'd been acutely disappointed to learn that he preferred boys over girls. But he'd harbored a real passion for the powerlift, treating it almost as if it were his personal gift to UNSA. Rock or steel or vanilla ice cream, he had said proudly—it made no difference to the powerlift. It would hold onto anything. During those few brief seconds of grinding behind her, the lift had sunk a pair of shafts into the floor and locked steel-alloy pins in place to anchor the cord. A self-activating motor would reset the pins if they loosened. *Funny*, she thought as her eyes searched for movement, *how things come back to you*.

"You first." Working quickly, Stone clipped the cord to Vikki's suit harness and retrieved the light.

"They're all around us, Stone."

"I know."

We're actually doing it, she thought wonderingly. *We're*

going deeper into this place. It's full of those slimy things, chock full of them, and how are we ever going to get out?

Drawing a breath, she got down on her hands and knees in the dust and grit and eased herself out over the edge. Bracing with one hand, she touched the controls on her belt and activated the powerlift. The cord spun out, then stopped with a jerk; she made a reflex grab for the lip of stone above her, banged her arm painfully against the rough wall, and cried out in pain.

"You okay?" Stone called from above.

"No," she snapped. "I just smashed my sounder. And I think my arm's bleeding."

"Need some help?"

"I'll live." Her hand went to the control belt. She drew a steadying breath and tried again. This time her touch was more delicate and the cord moved with only a slight lurch. She began descending toward the floor below. Halfway there she stopped and twisted around for a good, long look at the corridor below. No gray shadows scuttling about; no mewling, hissing, gurgling sounds. She glanced up at Stone, then activated the powerlift once more.

She reached the floor below and, after another quick look around with the light, sent the cord back up to Stone. A moment later his bulky form came over the edge and started down.

From the darkness behind her, far back in the tomb, she heard a scream of agony.

CHAPTER FIFTEEN

John Wheeler was deep inside the tomb when he heard the sound—a piercing cry of torment that made his blood freeze in his veins and his lips pull away from his teeth in an involuntary spasm of fear.

He had been in the tomb a long time, limping through the dusty gray corridors. He was not concerned about getting lost. Some instinct of orientation gave him firm assurance that each passageway was recorded inside him. He gave no thought to opening any of the small square crypts. He knew what they held. They were not for him. The mausoleum was vast, holding hundreds of thousands of decaying bodies. Those who had built the city were all dead, resting now in this dark place while the graceful spires they'd raised on the desert floor dissolved into dust; their tomb now gave shelter to a form of sublife that had not the slightest right of ownership.

But something remained. He felt its living presence around him and inside him, urging him on. Was it real, or was it only illusion? Even as he felt it stir inside him again, he was unsure. He had to find out.

The thing that had screamed was very close.

He stiffened as the sound came again: a screech of naked terror almost sensual in its intensity, drawing out into a high, keening cry of pain and despair. It rose above the other sounds, the scratchings and scrapings and mewlings that had become as much a part of the tomb as the gray stone and the dust. Then the scream was cut off with an abruptness that made Wheeler's scalp crawl. The mewling sounds changed, died away by degree, and were replaced by horrible gruntings and snufflings.

He listened to those new sounds for a long moment, frozen in place. The creatures were just around the corner from where he now stood, not far down the adjoining passageway. He switched off his light and felt the darkness draw in close like a shield. Then he edged forward, fingers trailing along the gritty wall for guidance. Warm, fetid air brushed his face as he reached the passageway. The grunting and snuffling sounds intensified, the scrabble of claws on the stone floor became frantic.

He flicked on his light and saw them: gray bodies turning, falling back in boiling frenzy, scattering away from the sudden glare. Reddened eyes gleamed briefly as one turned for a final backward glance. Then they were gone, leaving a cloud of dust and a corridor that was empty except for a single dark shape huddled against the wall.

Wheeler waited, his heart trip-hammering in his chest. The dark shape moved convulsively. He stepped forward for a closer look, and his stomach heaved. The dark shape was what was left of one of the creatures. It was small, one of the young. The others had fed on it—its face was gone, along with one upper limb. It lay twitching on the floor, not yet dead, dark fluid oozing across the gray stone.

Wheeler stepped back, drawing one quick breath after another, unable to take his eyes off the grisly scene.

Revulsion rose up and gagged him as full understanding came. It was a way of life for them. They had entombed themselves in this mound of rock where the only food was their own kind.

He turned and stumbled down the corridor, fleeing from the writhing, mangled body. It all came horribly clear. The dead city, the tomb, his own hopelessness. He stumbled over something and came to a shuddering stop. Was it all for this? Had all his years of searching led only to this?

No. He would not accept that.

He shook his head, wavering unsteadily, feeling a sudden compelling closeness to those who had brought the massive structure up from the desert floor those ages past. In the great scheme of design, in a universe filled with precise laws and inherent logic, it did not make sense to John Wheeler that those who had built the city should have died. That a plague or war or whatever had taken them should have done so seemed an outrageous injustice. He shared with them a kinship in futility. For them the search had ended. Whatever values they had sought, whichever set of illusions they had placed their faith and trust in—all had turned to dust.

He took a step forward, stumbled again, and looked down at a clutter of debris that was strewn across the floor. At some time in the past, the pressure had become too great, and the wall had fractured, spilling great chunks of rock and mortar out across the floor. Several vaults had been exposed, one of them directly in front of him. He swung his light up and looked inside. His blood ran cold. He stared at the dead thing inside the vault for a long time.

"No," he whispered. "Oh, no, no." Trembling, he switched off his light. The tomb waited, its silence mocking him. It had been waiting, waiting for him to see, to understand. Waiting to deal Wheeler the final blow. Its ancient life stirred inside him. Another vision came from the past: a sun hanging over a vast and bustling city, glistening off high, curving spires, softening into tones of red and brown—then the overwhelming despair rushed in on him.

Not his past this time, but *theirs*. His skin crawled.

Something scraped across a stone. A mewling sound from the darkness only a few meters in front of him was answered by another behind him. He realized that they had gathered close around him in the darkness.

Another sound: Cari's voice, misting toward him through a shifting, crackling past.

Suddenly the blackness was too great to tolerate, the sounds inside the tomb too filled with meaning. He pressed the switch on his light and blinked as its harsh glare filled the corridor. The tomb creatures crouched before him, bloated white faces twisted into horrible grins, bulging eyes regarding him with unblinking malevolence.

And understanding.

I will not run again. I will not.

He stepped forward. The gray shadows boiled and hissed. Then his lips drew back over his teeth. He drew his sizzler and hissed back.

The mewling rose to a shriek as they swarmed toward him.

CHAPTER SIXTEEN

Jack-a-dandy simmered under the white-hot sun. Inside, Oliver McElroy and Vito Cracchiolo sweated in a long silence that was broken only by the pod's soft whirrings and clickings and the rattle of sand against the metal skin. The desert glared at them through the open hatchway.

Time was running out. McElroy, in the control chair, alternated his gaze between the flickering vidscreen and the shifting lines of the sounder. The pattern on the sounder had changed a few minutes ago as one of the synchronized wrist units stopped emitting signals. From this distance, *jack-a-dandy* could not pinpoint which of the three had stopped.

McElroy felt the tension of indecision as he'd never felt it before. One of the sounders had been damaged. He wondered what had happened to the person wearing it.

He looked at the chronometer above the console, then back to the vidscreen. If Stone and Redford were coming back, they should have been on their way by now. A little over four hours remained in which to find Wheeler and get the spud tied back into *jack-a-dandy*'s drive system. His fingers drummed the arm of the control chair; four hours did not seem like a lot of time. A strong gust drove sand against the pod; a flurry of it came through the hatchway and peppered the back of his neck.

"We going after them, cap'n?" Cracchiolo asked, behind him.

"I don't know." McElroy felt as if he had spent half his life baking inside *jack-a-dandy*'s metal hull. He leaned back against the chair, looking up at the gray blankness of the ceiling. He could feel the movements of the pod against its stabilizers as the wind repeatedly slammed against it. He closed his eyes, thinking of all the codes and checks and confirmations that were supposed to prevent things like this from happening, and wondered if that sounder blinking out meant that one of his people was dead.

He sighed and opened his eyes. There really wasn't any choice. "Let's get into our lifesuits. We're going after them."

It did not take long to follow the sounder's directions through the ruined city to the tomb, and then to the fracture through which the others had gone before. Forty-five minutes after leaving *jack-a-dandy*, McElroy and Cracchiolo were worming their way through the fault into the tomb.

"Hey, cap'n, you know what? I don't like it in here." Cracchiolo's voice was strangely muted, as if he were afraid to speak too loudly lest he awaken the awful gods that surely dwelt in this place.

McElroy kept silent. He crouched under the broken ceiling, beaming his light along the way they would have to go. The fracture narrowed just ahead, the jagged rock splitting into a high arch and the walls closing in as if something had squeezed the massive boulders together and buckled them upwards. The smell was almost heady; something very large had crawled in here and died. But that was of no particular concern to McElroy. Dead things, he reasoned, were less dangerous than live things.

He moved forward again, wincing as pain splintered upward from his injured ankle. When he reached the place where the passageway twisted into a new direction, he stopped and cocked his head, listening.

The place did that. It made you hear sounds that weren't there, made you imagine shadowy movement where none existed. Common sense told him there was nothing to fear. All through the macabre jungle and the bare ruins of the city, they'd seen nothing that looked to be even remotely threatening. Whoever had built this place was long gone. He told himself that again, then drew a breath and began inching his way around the jagged splay of stone. This was no time for them to start getting jumpy. They couldn't afford to, not with three hours remaining until the drive engines went critical.

Halfway through, with his face pressed against the rough stone, his arms flat out against it for balance, he heard a small sound from Cracchiolo and turned to look. In the backwash of light Cracchiolo's eyes were wide and staring. *It's bad*, McElroy thought, *but it isn't that bad. Crackers looks as though he's seen a—*

Then he realized that Cracchiolo was not looking at him at all, but was staring past him into the twisting passageway that opened out beyond the corner. McElroy watched for a moment, fascinated by the way the look of stark terror played around Cracchiolo's eyes and mouth and the small muscles of his face. Then Cracchiolo's mouth widened, and strangling sounds came out.

McElroy turned his head to look into the passageway. It was not easy; wedged in as he was between the jutting stones, he was forced to move carefully to avoid scraping the skin off his cheek. Then he saw what Cracchiolo was staring at. Out in the passageway, hanging in the blackness twenty paces from where he stood between the boulders, was a swarm of glowing coals. He looked closer and suddenly knew what they were. His stomach knotted itself and adrenaline squirted, pulling all the strength from his legs.

The glowing coals were eyes. A family of them, swollen red things with tiny pupils like malignant warts staring at him, not blinking. Eyes with no souls behind them, surrounded by shapes only vaguely outlined in the darkness. McElroy's blood turned to ice water as he realized how thoroughly he and Cracchiolo were trapped here in this passageway. Faint sounds came now from those shadowy figures. The eyes moved closer. Behind him, Cracchiolo's breath rasped in and out.

McElroy twisted suddenly backwards, not even feeling the pain of his ankle banging against a stone as he fought to free the sizzler from his belt. The beam of his lantern swung around as shadowy forms scattered, clawed feet scrabbling against the stone floor. He caught a fresh whiff of the death-smell and knew that it was coming not from something that had died, but from something that was horribly alive.

His light flashed into an empty corridor.

They were gone. Only a drifting fog of dust and that overpowering stench of decaying flesh remained as testimony that they had been there at all.

"They're gone." Cracchiolo's voice was a harsh whisper.

McElroy steadied his light, training it along the fracture. The beam touched nothing but broken stones and drifting dust.

He swallowed and found his voice. "We have to keep moving." It was the last thing he wanted to do. Then he turned to look at Cracchiolo. "You okay?"

Cracchiolo's head moved in a brief negative gesture, not so much in answer to McElroy's question as in open wonder. "What were those things, cap'n?" Then: "Never mind. I don't want to know."

It wasn't so much the creatures that had unnerved them, McElroy knew, as the overall setting in which they found themselves. They were inside a massive stone ruin that did not look at all inviting. The death smell was all around, and there was no quick and easy escape. Taken together, it was a setting that invoked all the primitive fears of their race: the inherent dangers of darkness, superstitious fears of the unknown, the dread of confinement. All the horrors of humankind's ancient past rolled up together in a package guaranteed to speed up the pulse rate and set the hairs at the back of the neck on end. The creatures were merely a final touch.

McElroy braced himself against the load of those ancient fears and pushed ahead, squeezing between the jutting rocks to make his way down the sloping fissure with Cracchiolo close behind.

At last they emerged into a larger fault that, although anything but roomy, at least allowed them the relief of standing fully erect. McElroy's light stabbed through the darkness and found the hole Tom Stone had gouged through the crumbling wall.

Without giving himself time for fatal consideration of what might be waiting on the other side of that hole, he moved quickly across to it, scrambled through, and dropped to the floor. A moment later Cracchiolo followed.

They stood in wary silence for a long moment, looking about them, hunched under the low ceiling in a narrow corridor that stretched straight out away from them on either side. That they were inside the structure was evident. That there were other things in here with them was also evident. Sounds came from the darkness all around them. Sweat crept down McElroy's back under the thin fabric of his lifesuit. Never in his life had he felt so small and isolated.

"The sounder, cap'n," Cracchiolo said quietly. The skittering noises stopped at the sound of his voice, which was somehow far worse than if they had continued undisturbed.

McElroy looked down at his sounder. The dancing lights revealed the patterns of two distinct units within range: one not far ahead, another deep in the tomb. The more distant one would be Wheeler, the nearer would be Tom Stone or Vikki Redford.

He glanced at Cracchiolo, then set his light on wide angle and began moving down the corridor.

They passed the crypt Vikki and Tom had opened and, after a brief glance at what reclined inside, moved on. This was no time for sightseeing. The scrabbling sounds stayed with them, keeping to the darkness. They both had their sizzlers out, ready in case whatever was making those sounds decided to come up for a closer look.

It was not until they were nearly upon it that they saw the vertical shaft dropping away at the end of the corridor, with a powerlift clinging to its lip. McElroy stepped to the edge and trained his light down into the blackness. The shaft led to another level, another corridor stretching directly away from it.

"We're going to have to do it," he said to Cracchiolo.

"I know, cap'n."

McElroy knelt at the edge of the shaft, wincing at the pain that shot upwards from his ankle, and retrieved the dangling powerlift cord. Working briskly, he snapped the end fastener to a steel ring in his harness and climbed down over the edge. Bracing himself against the wall, he activated the powerlift and descended slowly to the floor below. After a quick survey of his surroundings, he sent the cord back up and watched while Cracchiolo hooked himself up, swung out over the edge with quick agility, and came down. They stood together, the wall of the shaft behind them, beaming their lights far out along a corridor that was exactly like the one they had left above: dust and stone, unadorned walls marked only by the faint outlines of row after row of square doors.

Definitely spooky, McElroy thought, as he drew a breath and stepped forward. He heard a brief scuffling sound behind him, then Cracchiolo's footsteps hurrying to catch up. He moved quickly along the corridor, favoring his bad ankle, flashing his light out ahead. An occasional check of his sounder assured him they were still on track of the others. The smell had returned—that putrid odor of dead fish—and the air had turned close and sour. His spine tingled.

The light caught something far ahead, blocking the corridor. A pile of rock debris, from the looks of it. His pace quickened. Cracchiolo's shuffling step followed close behind.

Closer now, he could see the obstruction more clearly. The ceiling had given way at some time in the past—perhaps thousands of years ago—dropping a load of boulders and broken stone onto the floor below. It had formed an effective barrier. They could not possibly get around it, not without digging away a good part of it. Which meant they would have to take one of the connecting corridors and try to work their way around it. . . .

Shuffling step?

A chilled finger traced its way down McElroy's spine. Cracchiolo was a springy walker. He never shuffled his feet. And he had those steel taps on the heels of his boots, the clack-clack that always irritated Vikki—

McElroy stood frozen, staring sightlessly at the pile of rubble. His mind went flying back over the past few minutes. He heard again the shuffling step, a dragging foot, a skittering sound like claws might make scratching along the gritty floor. And an earlier sound, heard at the bottom of the shaft and ignored—a brief, choked sob.

The shuffling had come to a stop behind him. It was Crackers, of course; Crackers, getting ready to say, "Come on, cap'n, we can climb over that little pile of dirt." Crackers, urging him forward with his incessant wisecracks. But Crackers said nothing, only stood there behind him, making a curious gurgling sound deep in his throat.

McElroy waited, transfixed, for something to happen. His legs were planted into the floor, the light held out before him in an iron grip. The sound behind him deepened—then came another shuffling step, another clicking of claws against stone.

Then, in a flash of revelation, McElroy understood. His mouth curved upward in a faint smile of relief.

That prankster, Crackers. He couldn't make himself be serious for long, even in a place like this. Crackers knew what was going through McElroy's mind, because the same things were going through his own. Too much had happened in the past few hours. They were strung out on fear, letting their imaginations run wild—and Crackers knew just what to do to cure them. He would give it all a light touch, ease up their fears by scaring McElroy half out of his wits by dragging one foot, scraping something—his lantern, probably—against the stone wall, wheezing and moaning like some dying thing.

Crackers, the eternal screw-off.

Well, if he could dish it out—

McElroy flicked his lantern to highest intensity and swung around to give it to Crackers-the-Clown full in the face. Halfway around, the death-smell hit him solidly and he knew he had made a horrible mistake. There was no way for Crackers to fake that smell. But it was too late to stop, too late to do anything but swing the lantern up and look at the thing that waited behind him.

CHAPTER SEVENTEEN

"Why is CommSec involved in this?"

"We've been having problems with Sierra communications. We were hoping this memorandum might help explain it."

Jahn Willson glanced briefly at the signature—his own—on the lower left corner of the tattered document. Then he looked up at Lars with a puzzled and slightly belligerent frown. "I don't see how it could. Did you get this from Bannat?"

Lars shook his head. "I found it in the operations library."

Willson's frown deepened. "This was supposed to go to Jack Bannat. Why was it in the library?"

Lars shrugged. He did not want to get involved in a discussion about how he had obtained the memorandum. "Routing error, I suppose."

"If you have a question about it, why aren't you following normal procedures?"

Lars realized then that Jahn Willson was not going to be put off so easily by the fabrication he had put together. He understood Willson's question well enough. If CommSec wanted information from the Blue, standard procedure called for a memo to be sent from Raymond Spick to Hans Claus, director of Field Reconnaissance. Claus or one of his assistants would follow up on the request with a direct reply to Spick. None of which was possible in this case because of Spick's directive that no other departments be involved.

"We're in a hurry for an answer on this," Lars answered, keeping his voice casual. "Mr. Spick thought we might be able to save time by coming directly to the source."

Willson looked at Lars, still cool and undecided. If the plan were going to fail, Lars knew, it would fail here. The Blue were not to be trifled with.

The research section of Field Reconnaissance was known as the Blue for the simple reason that it was the only department aboard *Graywand* with access to blue priority in emergency situations. Even *Graywand*'s executive staff held only green priority, which meant that in matters of research and reconnaissance those of the Blue had authority even over Captain Uriah, if they determined in their own minds that the situation called for it.

The arrangement was necessary because of the nature of the Blue's work—emergency situations required quick decisions without the fuss of committee action and supporting paperwork. But, at the same time, the arrangement also provided opportunities for those awkward power struggles that all good administrators wanted to avoid. Captain Uriah and Director Claus were both intelligent men and able administrators. Claus realized that while invoking blue authority to override Uriah's decisions was possible, it was clearly not something to be done without consideration. By the same standard, Captain Uriah, while recognizing the necessity for blue priority, had no desire to let situations develop which could result in Claus feeling it necessary to exercise his power. In the few cases of procedural disagreement that arose between *Graywand* administration and the research section, Uriah and Claus agreed mutually that a quiet discussion was preferable to an open conflict, and disagreements had always been resolved in that way.

But the mere fact that blue priority existed for them, added to the unique and often over-romanticized nature of their work, had the effect of setting the few dozen members of the Blue apart from the several thousand other personnel that comprised *Graywand*'s staff. The Blue almost never socialized with others. They had no contact with the rest of *Graywand* except as required for routine operations, and even then the association was kept on a formal basis. Their personal quarters and administrative offices occupied *Graywand*'s entire sixth level.

Lars Clemens, as one of many CommSec links on *Graywand,* had spoken to members of the Blue many times, but to the best of his knowledge had never come face to face with one until this meeting with Jahn Willson. He had been nervous and a little in awe from the time he'd stepped out of the elevator and walked hesitantly down the sixth-level corridor, searching for the data encoding room. He was a trespasser, violating territory that belonged to someone else.

He'd found Jahn Willson behind a terminal in a surprisingly austere cubby with the words DATA DOCUMENTATION–ENCODING stenciled on the graymetal door. Willson was dark and lean, with bushy eyebrows and narrow lips turned down in a permanent scowl. The scowl deepened now as Willson considered Lars's request.

"If you need the information today," he told Lars, "you should have submitted the request two days ago."

"It's really important," Lars urged, forcing his voice to remain calm even though his nerves were jangling. If Willson chose to verify Lars's request or, worse, to file a complaint with CommSec administration about the matter, it would mean not only the end of Lars's inquiry into the disappearance of McElroy and his crew, but also the end of Lars on *Graywand*. "We would not have come directly to you if we hadn't thought it of vital importance."

"Oh, never mind," Willson interrupted with distaste. He handed the memo across to Lars. "What do you want to know?"

Lars almost sighed with relief. "The circumstances, primarily. Why was the memo sent to Bannat in the first place?"

"Because he's the one that made the mistake. It's all in the report. Bannat found a ninety-nine and keyed in the wrong coordinates."

"The new planet was Tartarus?"

Willson nodded impatiently.

"Has it been developed?" Lars asked.

"Not yet. Takes a few months with funding and all that."

With those few words, Willson had verified Lars's greatest concern. McElroy and the others were stranded on an uninhabited planted. "How could Bannat enter the wrong coordinates?"

A small, tight frown crossed Willson's face. "You have to know Bannat. He's a good technician, but he's one of those guys who thinks he can carry everything he needs up here." Willson tapped the side of his head. His formal demeanor was beginning to ease. "Those research pods have brainpower you wouldn't believe, and Bannat has one of the newest models." He paused, then uttered what Lars guessed was, for him, a rare reflection on human nature. "Maybe Jack's intimidated by the notion of relying on a machine to keep track of what's happening. More likely, he's just stubborn. For whatever reason, he uses his own memory and little scraps of paper too much, and sometimes he gets himself into trouble. That's what happened here. When he found Tartarus, he jotted the coordinates down on a little scrap of paper and shoved it in a drawer. Then he picked up the wrong scrap when it came time to feed them to *Graywand*'s navigator and gave the navigator the coordinates for the ninety-nine he'd found just before Tartarus.''

"Sierra." It was all fitting into place.

"That's right. We learned about it when we sent our drone through the stream to Tartarus. Or rather, we thought we did. The drone received the message and bounced it back, exactly on schedule. Everything seemed okay. But when one of our field pilots made the initial test skip, she broke out on Sierra instead of Tartarus. Then she discovered that the drone had gone there as well. That's when the problem got dumped on me. I traced it back, found out how Bannat had fouled it up, and set up new coordinates for Tartarus. I sent this," he indicated the memorandum with a wave of his hand, "to Bannat so he could clear up his end of it."

"His end?"

"The old coordinates. Bannat set them up, so only he had the authority to remove them. One of NavSec's nuttier regulations, but it's a fact of life. I had no choice but to do it that way."

Human error. The final link made the connection. Jack Bannat never received the memorandum from Jahn Willson. With this single torn document stashed away and forgotten in a file drawer in *Graywand*'s operations library, Bannat had never suspected that anything was wrong.

And the old Tartarus coordinates had never been erased from the navigator's file.

Benjamin Hill scratched his beard and leaned back in his chair, propping his feet up on the cluttered workbench. He studied the Willson memorandum and slowly shook his head. "I don't see how it's possible for two planets to have the same coordinates. Those guys in the Blue, sometimes they go off the deep end."

"You think Willson's wrong?"

Hill frowned. "Anyone else, I'd say yes. But I've

crossed paths a time or two with Willson. He's a first-class jerk, but he knows his stuff."

"So we're back to the original question. How can two sets of coordinates occupy the same space in the navigator's files?"

Hill thought for a moment. "It isn't exactly like that." Then he thought some more and his face cleared. "No, not like that at all. I explained it that way earlier to keep it simple. But I didn't think it through all the way. Stream coordinates aren't really physical locations in the navigator's file. They're more like end-stops. When we want to make a skip, we tell the navigator which coordinates we've assigned to the target. It scans its memory until it matches them up, then grabs the information stored there."

"Information it needs to compute the characteristics for the skip."

"Right."

More pieces fell into place. "The coordinates are only a flag. If you had two planets stored under the same set of coordinates—" Lars paused, fumbling with an unwieldy concept. "—you'd have two flags in two separate areas of memory. Two sets of coordinates with the same name. You'd stand a fifty-fifty chance of hitting either set when you called up the coordinates."

Hill considered this with a doubtful frown. "Yes, I suppose that's what would happen. *If* you could have a duplicate set of coordinates in the first place. Which is impossible, because the navigator checks for things like that."

"It does?" Lars felt his carefully constructed picture falling into ruin. "How?"

"It scans for duplicates when the coordinates are first entered. It would reject them—" Hill stopped abruptly, the corners of his mouth drawing down. "No, that isn't right. During data input, the navigator can't reject what it's given. It can only point out errors. It can't fix them." The thought seemed to spur him on. He moved suddenly, swinging his feet to the floor with a thump and leaning forward to his console. After keying in a brief command, he looked up at the information that began flowing across his readout screen.

"It can't be," he muttered after a moment. He keyed in a command and studied another stream of information. Then he leaned back in his chair and looked bleakly at Lars.

CHAPTER EIGHTEEN

As the light caught the creature full in the face, the first thing McElroy saw was the blood smeared across the gaping orifice that served as its mouth, running in thick rivulets over its scaly chin. It was nearly as large as a man, with dead tissue hanging off its fish-white skin in folds. It reared up on a double pair of spindly legs to look straight at McElroy, tiny dark pupils swimming in the center of each bloated eye.

McElroy took a step back, stumbled over shards of stone and nearly fell, but did not because he could not allow himself to fall with that hunched-over thing taking yet another step toward him. It stared straight into the light, seemingly mesmerized by the powerful beam. Its hands came up, shriveled white things with four-inch talons. The razor edges caught the light, and McElroy saw the rest of it: hairless belly, swollen tight; multijointed limbs; lidless eyes, staring.

McElroy took another stumbling step backward. He

groped for his sizzler, brought it up, and squeezed off a quick crackling blast of energy. The creature screamed, spraying McElroy with bloody froth. Black fluid gushed from the charred stub of an upper limb. The creature screamed again, a high-pitched shriek of rage and agony.

Then McElroy erupted into sudden motion, throwing himself sideways into the wall, spinning away frantically, and somehow avoiding those grasping talons as he ran headlong down the corridor. The beam of light bounced wildly ahead of him.

He did not see the thing lying in the middle of the corridor until his foot snagged on it and he went sprawling, cracking the side of his head hard. The lantern bounced and clattered on the floor but mercifully did not go out. He scuttled after it, clutched it in one fist, and spun around to face the horror behind him. But it wasn't there. He'd outdistanced it. The corridor was empty. Almost.

Empty except for the dark shape he had stumbled over, a formless heap lying in the middle of the corridor like a pile of dirty laundry. He scrambled over to it, feeling nothing as strong as the need to get away from this place. The huddled shape wore a brown lifesuit. He reached out a hand. "Crackers—"

He tugged on a shoulder, and the body flopped toward him. His light fell across the place where Cracchiolo's face should have been, and he saw raw flesh, shards of white bone, empty eye sockets oozing gray stuff held together by white stringy filaments.

He fell back, vomited, and came up gasping for air.

Then he heard the creature mewling its way down the corridor like some monstrous cat. He grabbed for his sizzler, and realized that he no longer had it. Then he was running. Something up ahead—the end of the corridor. He pounded toward it, the sounds of the creature coming up close behind him.

He was under the shaft, groping wildly for the hanging cord, looping the handle of his light through one arm and frantically pulling himself up hand over hand because there was no time to fool with the powerlift control, no time at all—

He almost made it.

But the terrible thing was below him in the darkness, wheezing, gurgling, mewling softly—sure in the knowledge that it had him.

Something closed over his ankle and gave a powerful tug.

"You ever wonder why the Blue get such fat paychecks, Stone? I'll tell you why. Because they get paid to take risks like this. They're trained for it, and they have the fancy equipment and the big guns, and they're the ones who ought to be out here. Not us. Not a bunch of auditors."

"Uh-huh," Stone agreed absently.

"Well, I think we ought to make sure whoever's responsible for this screwup gets called on it. It isn't right that incompetent asses get put in positions where they can do things like this. *Graywand*'s management needs an overhaul, from the ground up. The whole bunch ought to be thrown out and replaced."

"Yeah." Stone paused for a moment, studying something his light revealed far ahead. Vikki, peering around his shoulder, saw nothing. After a moment, Stone hunched his shoulders slightly and moved on. They had seen no more of the creatures since descending the shaft to the lower level. *Small favors,* Vikki thought bitterly.

"Doesn't it even bother you that we're going through all this because somebody on *Graywand* screwed up?" she went on. "I mean, what if—what if—" *What if we don't get out of here alive,* she had almost said. But suddenly, even thinking those words made her realize she would not like the sound of them spoken aloud. She swallowed a momentary surge of panic and amended her statement: "What if they do something worse next time?"

"Something could be worse than this?" Stone glanced down at the sounder on his wrist, then stopped so abruptly that Vikki bumped into him.

"What are you *doing*?"

"Something's wrong." He tapped the instrument, frowning as he watched the flickering patterns of light. Two more sounders had come within range. "Must be Crackers and Roy." He glanced up at her, turned to look down the corridor. "Doesn't make sense, all of us wandering around down here, getting each other's signals mixed up." He consulted the sounder again, then made up his mind. "Let's keep after Wheeler. No sense going back now."

"Wonderful."

Her tone made him turn. "You okay?"

"Oh, just fine," she replied acidly. "Haven't enjoyed myself so much since, gosh, can't remember when."

Stone gave her a puzzled look, then hitched up his pack and moved down the corridor.

This was it, Vikki told herself bitterly, following behind. If she got out of this in one piece, she was leaving the agency. Forget Field Recon. Forget the Blue. Forget UNSA altogether. All the times she'd said it before, she had never meant it with the certainty she felt now.

She shivered as the sounds started up again. They were worse now, and they came from the darkness all around them. The message was clear. *Get out, get out, get out. This is our place, not yours.*

"You can have it," she said to the gray walls.

Throbbing pain. Rough stone against his face. Distant sounds of alien life. Sickening odor of decay.

Blackness.

McElroy opened his eyes. Or thought he did. He closed them again. Opened them. There was no difference.

I'm blind, he thought.

He sat up and grimaced with pain as he straightened his right leg. The throbbing in his ankle subsided to a dull ache. Nothing broken at least. He rose to his feet, bumped into a wall, and leaned against it gratefully, trying to keep the tingling feel of panic at bay, listening to the distant mumblings far back in the tomb. He had to concentrate on what he knew, tune out all the irrelevant details, because even in his disoriented state he knew that whatever slim chance of survival he had depended on organized thinking. Fact one: He was alive. Fact two: He was blind.

Somehow, fact two was the more difficult to accept. He reached up, touched his eyelids to make sure they were open, and caught a faint glow of light from his moving arm. The sounder, lights flickering across its tiny screen. Fact two amended: He wasn't blind. He was in a place that was pitch black. Alive and not blind. *Good, McElroy. What else?*

Fact three: He was inside the tomb with no sizzler and no light. Not so good. And from that emerged the first order of business. Find the lantern. But do it calmly. No scrambling around, bashing his head against the wall, falling over rocks. None of that would do any good. An organized search was called for.

It's broken. If it weren't broken, it would still be on.

Maybe so, he argued, but maybe not. Maybe when the lantern fell, it hit the floor in such a way as to push the switch to the off position. *Never mind the maybes, just find it.*

Keeping the stone wall within touching distance, he fanned his arms out in front of him to brush the floor. Nothing. He inched forward on his knees and repeated the brushing motion. His hand touched something cold and sticky, something with the texture of rotting flesh. He snatched his hand away and skittered backwards, swallowing the bile that rose in his throat. He bumped into a wall and pressed against it while his heart pounded and his breathing rattled in his throat.

God, he needed a match, a candle, anything—

He realized what it was that lay there on the corridor floor. Even before the chase down the corridor, the creature had lost a fair amount of its life-fluid through the blackened stump of its upper limb. Yanking McElroy down from the powerlift cord must have exhausted its last ounce of strength.

McElroy swallowed. The creature was dead. He had to get a hold on himself, find the light and the sizzler before more of those gray nightmares came to find their brother.

Again he leaned forward and swept his hands across the floor. Blinking against the rising dust, he moved along on his knees, feeling for the lantern. Except for a sharp stone he located painfully with his knee, he encountered nothing.

He fought down his panic, forced the trembling in his arms to cease, and tried again, this time going as far as the wall at the end of the corridor before giving up. The lantern had to be here. He sat back on his heels against the wall and collected himself. The creature had attacked, and he'd dropped the lantern in his fall from the shaft. It should be right here.

He started back down the corridor and had not gone three meters when his groping hand bumped the lantern. His fingers closed over it; he went limp with relief. The switch—

The handle was smashed. The entire switch mechanism and power unit had broken away.

Stay calm, he commanded himself. Only another fact: The lantern was broken. Now was the time for a decision. Not too difficult, since he was faced with only two alternatives. He could use the powerlift to pull himself up the shaft and, by following the corridor to the fracture in the wall, would quite possibly be able to find his way out of here. If he didn't encounter any tomb creatures on the way. Or he could follow the pulsing lights of the sounder, feel his way through the narrow passageways, and perhaps be lucky enough to find Tom Stone and Vikki Redford. If he did not step into an open shaft, or fall over something and knock himself senseless. Or run into any tomb creatures. He did not care much for that alternative. He did not like being inside the tomb without a light. The darkness here was absolute, the kind one did not even think about, lest the mind conjure up too many horrors to fill it. There were plenty of horrors in this place already without adding more.

But Oliver McElroy did not want to die. Not just yet, not with another forty or fifty years ahead of him, not with a wife and kids and a good career with UNSA waiting for him. Especially not in this place. And he would most certainly die if *jack-a-dandy*'s drive engines blew. All of them would.

So, he made his decision and forced himself not to think about it any more as he began feeling his way along the gritty wall. Distant scuffling sounds came from the blackness ahead.

CHAPTER NINETEEN

"You did *what*?" Robert Spalding asked incredulously.

"I found out what happened to McElroy and his crew. They're on a planet called Tartarus."

"You spoke to NavSec? And the Blue?" Spalding seemed to be having a hard time speaking. He sat rigidly in the high-backed chair behind his desk, palms flat on the polished metal surface. "Mr. Spick ordered that the matter be kept strictly within CommSec."

"What happened was not a CommSec error. That's what I've been trying to tell you."

This had a slight calming effect. "Whose error was it?"

Lars hesitated before answering. Even knowing Spalding as he did, even being aware that Spalding's top priorities were to protect himself and CommSec, Lars was nevertheless surprised. "Mr. Spalding, it seems to me that the important thing now is to ask the Blue for help. McElroy and his people have been on an undeveloped planet nearly ten hours—"

"But it *is* a ninety-nine."

"Yes, sir."

"McElroy's been around awhile. He can take care of himself." Spalding relaxed slightly, leaning forward to fold his hands in front of him on the desk. "What we have to do now is piece together what happened. Now that you've stirred it up, Spick will have to take it to Uriah. He'll want to know the facts first."

More wasted time. But there was nothing to do but play it Spalding's way. More argument would only use up more time. Lars described Jack Bannat's discovery of the new planet and the subsequent error in conveying coordinates to *Graywand*'s navigator. Spalding's brow lowered with incomprehension as Lars explained the significance of two sets of coordinates existing in the navigator's file—one providing the k-stream characteristics for Sierra and the other for Tartarus.

"Don't they have ways to check for that?" Spalding interrupted.

"Yes, sir. The navigator responded with an error message when the encoding clerk entered the duplicate set of Sierra coordinates."

"Well, then?"

"She was a temporary from another department, filling in for someone else. She wasn't fully trained in NavSec procedure. Instead of following up immediately on the error message, she wrote a note to the encoding room supervisor." Lars remembered Benjamin Hill's explosive reaction when he finally located the tracks of the encoding error in the Sierra data file and reconstructed what had happened. NavSec had strict regulations concerning error messages during input. They were to be referred to the encoding room supervisor for immediate disposition. When located and questioned, the substitute clerk, nearly in tears over Hill's wrath, admitted that she had heard something about dealing with data entry errors, but the supervisor had stepped out for a moment, and the clerk, already behind schedule in a job that was unfamiliar to her, thought it would be more practical to leave the supervisor a note and continue with her work. "The note was lost, and the clerk forgot all about it."

"So the navigator accepted the duplicate set of coordinates?"

Lars nodded. "It's only programmed to issue an error message. It'll continue with the job if it's instructed to do so. Since nine out of ten encoding problems are due to operator errors, the people at NavSec decided they could save time by overriding at the data entry level. I think they're going to change that now."

"I should think so," Spalding said with satisfaction. Another peg in NavSec's coffin. "But you and McElroy confirmed coordinates to Sierra. How could those coordinates send them to this other place?"

"Because the coordinates aren't the key. The k-stream characteristics stored with those coordinates give the real directions for the skip. When we confirmed coordinates, we didn't realize we were actually confirming two sets, one for Sierra and one for the other planet, Tartarus. When McElroy's pod skipped, the navigator happened to hit the set that held the directions to Tartarus."

Spalding considered this. "Sierra was established several months ago. If there were problems with the coordinates, why haven't they come up before now?"

Lars glanced at the chronometer on his wrist, then sighed inwardly and launched into the more complex story behind the dual sets of coordinates. The same question Spalding raised had also bothered Benjamin Hill. By the law of averages, at least half the skips meant for Sierra should have gone instead to Tartarus. It did not make sense that, of all the skips made in recent weeks to Sierra, McElroy's pod was the first to be sidetracked to Tartarus.

Hill had thought about it a long time, muttering under his breath and filling several sheets of paper with rough diagrams before finding the answer. The navigator, he'd explained to Lars, stored the bulk of its information, including k-stream coordinates and attendant stream characteristics, in a separate processor that was in effect composed of several thousand linear storage cells. Each cell was capable of holding thousands of pieces of information. The original Sierra coordinates were stored near the center of one of those cells. When the duplicate set was entered, it fell into an area near the end of another cell.

"I don't get it," Spalding said. "Why would that make a difference?"

"When the navigator needs a set of coordinates, it scans the processor cells until it finds them, then pulls out the data it needs. With the correct coordinates at the center of a cell, and the duplicate set in a remote area near the end of another cell, the chance of hitting either of the two sets at the time of a skip was taken out of the fifty-fifty range. The coordinates stored near the center of the cell—the Sierra set—were most often the first to be found by the scanner. It was usually in their general area when it began looking. The Tartarus coordinates were farther back, with the coordinates of other new planets, none of which have been cleared by the Blue."

Spalding's face showed a glimmer of comprehension. "So those coordinates aren't often called up."

"That's right. Unless the Sierra coordinates were requested immediately after a request for coordinates in one of those outlying cells, the first set it would find would be the right ones."

That explained something else, Lars realized suddenly. When McElroy first contacted him after the skip, the navigator's scanner was still locked into the Tartarus coordinates, so the commbox functioned properly. But between the time of that call and the time Lars tried to contact McElroy a few minutes later, the scanner was called away from the Tartarus coordinates for another skip or commbox transmission. When it scanned from its new location, it found the correct coordinates for Sierra. Lars, unable to contact McElroy at those coordinates, had assumed that McElroy's commbox was malfunctioning.

"It's their fault," Spalding said, leaning back in his

chair with an I-knew-it-all-along look on his face. "Right down the line, NavSec and the Blue. Heads will roll over this, I promise you." Then his eyes narrowed as he thought of something else. "Now that you know where he is, have you tried to contact McElroy to see if everything's all right?"

Lars nodded. "So far I haven't been able to get through."

"Why not?"

"I don't know. The signal's getting through. They aren't acknowledging."

Spalding's brow came down in sudden doubt. "You're sure you have all this straight? You're certain they're at this place you said?"

"Tartarus. Yes, I'm sure."

Spalding looked at him a moment longer, then pushed himself away from his desk and stood up. *At last,* Lars thought with relief, coming quickly to his feet. *At last some action.*

"Get your documentation together," Spalding said briskly. "We'll go over it with Spick when he gets back tomorrow."

Lars stiffened. "Tomorrow?"

"That's when he's due back from *Ysola.* I'll see that we get an early appointment." Spalding shook his head. "He is not going to be happy about this, Lars. I can tell you that. His instructions were clear."

"Mr. Spalding—"

Spalding waved a hand. "Don't worry about it. I'll see what I can do to smooth it out."

"Mr. Spalding, we can't wait until tomorrow. They could be in serious trouble out there."

"All the more reason to make sure we don't fly off the handle. If we went into a panic each time something didn't go just right, we'd never accomplish anything. I'm sure you understand that."

Lars shook his head. "I don't understand at all. We know where they are. We know they may be in danger.

The Blue could be there within the hour. I don't understand why we aren't trying to help them.''

"We'll get it straightened out when Spick gets back,'' Spalding assured him. "Don't worry.''

Don't worry. Lars pushed back his chair and stood up. A lot of him had drained away during those past few minutes. He felt weak and shaky.

"By the way,'' Spalding called after him as he reached the door. "Where'd they come up with the name Tartarus?''

Lars jabbed a thumb at the plate and the door slid open. He turned back to Spalding. He'd asked Willson the same question. "Field Recon stole the name from one of the old Terran religions. Tartarus is another name for Hell.''

CHAPTER TWENTY

For Tom Stone and Vikki Redford, the search for Wheeler was becoming frustrating.

They had been wandering through the narrow corridors for what seemed like hours, following the directions of the sounder on Stone's wrist but somehow never closing the distance to Wheeler. Now the sounder showed Wheeler to be somewhere to their right, and for twenty minutes they had been caught in a long corridor that stretched straight ahead into distant blackness without a single intersecting passageway that could take them in that direction.

They had seen no more of the tomb creatures; the only evidence of their existence were distant sounds and the ever-present smell of decay. Vikki had grown almost accustomed to them. Even the screaming claustrophobia she'd felt earlier had diminished to a sharp-edged tension. The frustration of tracking down Wheeler had a balancing effect on all her other worries. Which was why she stopped when she saw the door.

It was standing slightly ajar, larger than the little square crypts, almost begging to be opened. It appeared to have been carved from the solid stone of the wall. Tom walked past it without noticing, which did not surprise Vikki, because Tom Stone could blunder past a stampeding brontosaurus and never know it.

She stopped, caught by the dark crack between the wall and the edge of the door. It seemed horribly out of place—an actual door, nearly large enough for her to pass through without stooping. And it was in the right side of the corridor, opening perhaps into another corridor that could lead them toward Wheeler. She almost called out to Stone, then thought, *Why bother, just a quick look first. No sense getting Stone all jumpy over nothing.*

So, while Tom Stone clumped on down the corridor with the dust wisping up around his boots and his pack jouncing on his large shoulders, Vikki stepped to the door and gave it a tentative shove. It swung inward with a dry, rasping sound. She beamed her light inside. A narrow passageway with a low ceiling ran a short distance before branching off to the right.

Into another corridor?

She hesitated, conscious of Stone's footsteps ringing hollowly far down the outer corridor. She swallowed, wanting to take those few steps to the next juncture but unwilling to leave the open door.

She shook her head at her own uneasiness. It was only a few steps. And if she could find a passageway leading toward Wheeler—

She stepped inside and, stooping under the low ceiling, made her way to the next intersection. Another short passageway ended at another closed door. She shook her head. No way was she taking another step into this place. Not without Stone beside her. As she turned to go, she heard a hoarse scream.

She froze as a blade of ice scraped along her spine. The scream came again from somewhere behind the closed door. This time it was a long, drawn out "*Nooo*," and she

knew it was Wheeler. Somewhere close, maybe just behind that door.

She swallowed dry air, felt blood pulsing thickly in her
ears, and in the space of a heartbeat realized that Stone
was too far down the corridor to go after him now, not
with Wheeler being attacked by tomb creatures or fleshless
mummies or whatever other lovelies this place held to its
bosom. She gripped her sizzler, placed a foot against the
stone door, and pushed. It screeched open. A rush of air,
thick with that putrid odor of death, flowed past her,
funneling out through the new opening she'd created. Something rasped dryly behind her. She spun around as the door
to the outer corridor swung closed. By the time she reached
it, it was flush against the wall and solidly in place.

Oh, Lord—

Stay calm, she told herself, nearly gagging on the panic
that bubbled up inside her. *Just stay calm. You have a
weapon, and Stone is nearby, and besides, if the door
closed that easily, then it ought to just open right back up
again. Stay calm, stay calm,* stay calm. *Don't think about
all those tridees you've seen where the heroine steps into
the haunted house like some brainless female, and the
door swings shut, and out steps this dead thing with
groping hands—*

She turned back to the corridor, sizzler ready. No gray
shapes, no scrabbling sounds, no high-pitched mewlings.

Fine. Nerves all under control now. Yes.

She set the light for widest dispersion and propped it
against the wall. Then she put her weight against the door
and pushed. No effect. She may as well have been pushing
against solid rock. She stepped back and studied the faint
outline in the wall. The door fit perfectly, leaving only the
tiniest crack. It opened inward, she remembered, which
meant she would have to find a way to pull on it to get it
open. Which would be difficult, because whoever had put
it here had not thought about installing small conveniences
like handles.

After a nervous glance behind her, she pulled the pack

over her shoulders, dropped it on the floor, and began looking through it for something to use as a prybar. She was pleased in a jittery kind of way that her fingers trembled only slightly. She found the small, flat tool used for tightening the bolt on the powerlift fastenings. She slipped it into the crack between the door and the wall and worked with it for several minutes before it snapped into two pieces without having even budged the door.

Fine, she said to herself, stepping back. *Stone will come back. He'll get me out of here. All he has to do is push the door open. Even Stone ought to be able to manage that.*

She heard something behind her and spun around. Then she remembered why she had come here in the first place. "John? Are you there?"

Her voice came back to her in an eerie echo that discouraged another shout. Holding the light in one clenched fist and the sizzler in the other, she stepped cautiously to that door she'd kicked open and looked through into another narrow corridor. Ten meters away it branched off in two directions. After a moment she drew a jittery breath and paced off that ten meters and found that each adjoining corridor ran only a short distance before branching again.

She had seen something like this in an amusement park once. *Step into the House of Fun, kiddies.*

Not this time. She was not going a step farther. She had made one stupid mistake by coming in here in the first place; she would not compound it by wandering around and getting lost. Stone would be coming back any minute. She wanted to be right here waiting for him when he pushed open that door.

She returned to the outer wall and, after another brief search for a way to open the massive door, gave up in disgust and sat down on the floor with her back to the wall. She hugged her knees to her chest and wondered what would happen to her next.

* * *

"Vikki?"

Stone beamed the light back along the corridor. No answer. Something had gotten her, was his first thought. One of those gray shapes had taken her so quickly that he had not heard a thing. But that didn't seem possible. She had been not ten paces behind him. And Vikki was not someone to be taken quietly; there would have been at least the sound of a scuffle, and the signs of it in the heavy layer of dust on the floor.

The floor—he studied it with sudden realization. The tracks of their boots were clearly outlined in the thick dust.

He backtracked, and in a matter of seconds found the place where his single set of footprints had struck off down the corridor. Almost immediately he saw the faint outline of the door in the gray wall. He studied it closely under the light. This was not a crypt; it was much too large for that. It was a door, leading to another part of the tomb. Vikki's footprints ended here, which could only mean that for some reason she had gone through that door.

He gave the door a tentative push, then placed a shoulder against it and put his substantial weight behind it. The door was made of solid stone and, as he'd expected, showed not the slightest inclination to move. He stepped back and studied the footprints again. There was no doubt; Vikki was in there somewhere.

He slung the pack off his shoulder, then hunkered down on his heels in front of the door and began thinking about how to get it open.

Vikki glanced at the lighted dial of her chronometer and saw that only ten minutes had passed since she had decided to wait for Stone. It had been the longest ten minutes of her life. She sat motionless on the hard floor, her back against the wall, the light flaring out in front of her— waiting in the absolute silence that had mecifully maintained itself since that last sobbing gasp she'd heard from deep inside the maze of corridors.

She had spent most of that ten minutes staring down the

narrow passageway, thinking about Wheeler. *Yes,* she admitted to herself, *even worrying about the scrawny jerk.* After all the times she'd wished he would go somewhere and get lost, now more than anything she wanted to see him coming down that corridor toward her. Even his foolish smile would be a welcome sight. She licked her lips, remembering the hoarse cry, the strangled gasp. She did not expect to see John Wheeler again.

Silence.

Suddenly the thought of spending another minute on her hams in this horrid place was more than she could bear. She got to her feet awkwardly, muscles already stiff and sore, and moved down to the first intersection. She stood there and listened, her light glaring along the short expanse of gray stone.

Empty. Silent.

After a moment, she moved cautiously to the partially open door and pushed it fully open, sizzler steady in her hand. The light from her powerful lantern cut through the darkness. No shadowy movement, no scrabble of claws. She gave the door a firm push, shoving it far back against the wall, then stepped through. This would be a dandy place to get lost.

Then something else occurred to her. If the passageways kept splitting like this, the rightmost angles might eventually lead back to the outer corridor. If there was one open door for a fool like her to step through, why not another? If she kept to the right at each branch, she could not get lost. If she were unable to find a way out, she could always come straight back by simply keeping the wall always to her left.

Simple.

So don't stand here thinking about it. Do it.

She drew a breath to steady her nerves, all her senses screaming at her to go back, and started down the rightmost passageway. She moved warily, stopping often to listen to the silence around her and beam the light back the way she had come. She passed a half-dozen intersections of double or triple convergences, each time keeping faithfully to the rightmost branch.

Halfway down one of these short passageways, she stopped suddenly. She listened, not breathing, and had nearly convinced herself that the tiny sound had been only the workings of her imagination, when it came again—a soft rustle from the passageway ahead, from one of the angled branches the beam of light could not penetrate.

"John?" Her voice was a harsh whisper. The rustling sound stopped. Fear took a paralyzing grip on her as a low growling sound from the passageway grew into a high-pitched mewling. She took a step backwards, the flesh crawling at the base of her skull.

Then, suddenly, they were there—two of them, scuttling toward her like crabs down the corridor, gray bodies pressed low to the floor, mewling and hissing.

The sizzler crackled in her hand. Blue fire kicked up a wavering trail of dust across the floor. She gripped the weapon with both hands, trying to steady it, her thumb pressed rigidly against the firing stud. A blackened stripe smoked across the back of the nearest creature. It rose up screaming, caught the blue fire full in its throat and crumbled to a lifeless heap, oozing black fluid. The other one leaped, hissing, straight for Vikki's face. The sizzler crackled, flinging blue pulses into its swollen abdomen. The creature burst, spattering black gore across the floor. Something landed at Vikki's feet with a moist splat.

She screamed, then turned and plunged down the passageway, running headlong with no regard for the many twists and turns, wanting only to get as far away from that place as possible. A part of her realized that, if there were more of them, they could take her easily from behind, but she was powerless to do anything but run, choking on panic and dust, the beam of light bouncing wildly ahead of her.

When she stopped at last, whimpering, spinning around

to face whatever had come after her, the corridor behind was empty. She leaned against the wall, gasping for air.

Then she realized with a sickening jolt that her carefully thought-out plan had gone awry. In her panic, left and right had had no meaning. She had no idea how to get back to that outer corridor. She was lost.

CHAPTER TWENTY-ONE

Stone sat up straighter as an idea formed. He twisted around, training his light on the opposite wall. Solid rock. He studied it for a moment, thinking. Maybe.

Working quickly, he opened his pack and took out the two remaining powerlifts. He opened one, leaving the cord wound in its reel, and moved toward the gray wall opposite the door Vikki had gone through. *This cannot work,* a voice said inside him, but he squelched it and pressed the powerlift against the wall, holding it there as it came to life and drilled its twin shafts and locked itself in place. Leaving the cord dangling, he stepped across the corridor to attach the other powerlift to the center of the door. *It might work,* he told that inner voice. *It just might.* He reeled out the cords, doubled them on each side, and tied them together with a triple safety knot.

The cords were not breakable, the techs said. They'd take anything you could give them. Once, the story went, Nathan Blackaby of the Blue had used two powerlift cords to tow a sector ship away from an erratic breakout zone. They would not break.

"Let's hope for once they're right," Stone muttered aloud. He checked his knot, then used his control belt to activate the powerlift attached to the wall. He stepped well clear as the slack was taken up and the cord drew taut.

Fingering the knob, he eased the powerlift motor along at its lowest speed. The motor whined, then dropped in pitch and began pulling in earnest against that massive door. The cord became as rigid as a steel bar. The stone of the wall groaned and popped, spewing dust and fine particles out into the corridor. Stone licked his lips, his eyes glued to the unmoving door. "Pull," he urged the powerlift. *"Pull."*

The motor died with a sound like a small thunderclap. A puff of black smoke wisped toward the ceiling as the cord shuddered and went limp.

"Damn!" The techs were right. The cord did not break. It was the motor that couldn't take the strain.

Then he noticed the dark line around one edge of the door. Crossing the corridor in two quick steps, he ran his fingers around that dark line, half expecting to find that it was only a trick of the light. But it was real, all right. The door had given ground. Not much—less than a centimeter. But it had moved.

And Stone had one functioning powerlift left.

The creatures were closing in on her. She heard their scratchings and scrapings, the obscene mewling sounds they made to one another in the dark maze of passageways. She stood at a juncture with her back flat against the wall, her light set on wide dispersion so she could look down the three passageways that met here. She did not know what she was waiting for. She knew only that she could not take a step into any of the passageways with those things scuttling around in the darkness. Tears of frustration gathered in her eyes. She brushed them away angrily.

The creatures kept to the darkness, fleeting shadows far back in the dark corridors. They would never take her alive, she thought, as more tears gathered to blur her vision. That was one promise to herself she intended to keep. Her sizzler wouldn't be much good against them when they finally decided to come after her, not with them pouring out from all three directions at once, as they would surely do. But one short blast of the sizzler would be enough for what she had in mind. And this, she thought, squeezing out the tears, was a lousy place to die, in this stinking place with all those slimy things out there waiting. Not quite what Mr. and Mrs. Redford would have wanted for their little girl.

Sudden commotion in the central passageway—a blur of gray far back in the shadows as the creatures scattered down connecting corridors.

She shrank back against the wall as something lurched closer—a scarecrow moving jerkily on two stick legs, dust swirling up around its shuffling feet—a shambling boogeyman from the black depths, come for the final glory. Its gray eyes fastened on hers as she tried to press herself into the stone at her back. Then she looked closer.

"John?" she whispered. "John, is that you?"

His lifesuit was shredded and soaked with blood. One arm hung limp at his side, twisted at an unnatural angle. The entire left side of his face was a pulpy mass of blood and tissue. "John, for God's sake—"

"We've found them out, Vikki." The words that came from the torn lips were slurred, but they were spoken calmly. Wheeler reached out with his good hand and gripped her shoulder with surprising strength. "They're monsters, Vikki. In the fullest sense of the word. The worst kind of monster. They go against everything that is right and natural."

"John, you're hurting me."

"They do not like trespassers," Wheeler said. "They hate me. They know I can see inside their black souls." He laughed suddenly, a high, thin sound. Bloody froth bubbled at his lips. "Ah, yes, Vikki, I know them. I surely do."

She twisted away from him, her flesh crawling. She thought briefly of getting the medikit out of her pack, but realized that it would be pitifully inadequate. Wheeler needed to get to *Graywand*'s hospital facilities.

"It has all come together," he said, wavering unsteadily before her. "Just as it was meant to. Yes, exactly as planned." His bloody lips formed a grotesque, one-sided smile. "All these years, Vikki. All these years I've searched for something worth hanging onto. Something of value, that's all I wanted. That's all that kept me going, knowing that someday I would find it, knowing I was headed there."

"We have to get out of here, John. Can you—?"

He laughed again, cutting her off. "I didn't see it, Vikki. Blind, I guess, but I just didn't see it. They showed me. The vaults, they're full of them. The ones who built the city. And you know what, Vikki?" He threw back his head and laughed again. The sound of it sent a cold chill down her spine. "They're the same ones. *The same ones.*" He waved his arm out toward the moving shadows. "They've moved to the tomb. They built the city, and they were so beautiful. I felt them all around me, Vikki. Those who turned the wasteland into a beautiful city. I felt them, just as all my life I've felt that sense of lost values. I felt them but all the time what I felt was the past. It's where I've been all my life. Always a step behind, never quite in the *here* but always following in the *what was* and *what should have been*. They came here from the city—all of them, the living and the dead came here to rot in the same grave." He turned and looked down at her. A torn piece of flesh hung just below the bloody pit where his right ear should have been. "These creatures—they're the ones who did it, Vikki. They told me so. They built the city, then ran away from it. It was too beautiful for them."

She shook her head, confused. She saw again that shriveled body inside the crypt Stone had opened. The tomb creatures—yes, Wheeler could be right—they could be the same. She felt a chill. *"They told me so . . ."* She remembered the feeling she'd had earlier, a feeling that she was being watched, an alien touch inside. Was it possible Wheeler had really communicated with these monsters? She shuddered. "That doesn't matter, John. We have to get out of—"

"Values." He was crying now, horrible sounds from deep in his throat. "That's all I wanted. Something to make my joke of a life worthwhile. I found it here, Vikki. I knew I would, and I was not disappointed." Even with the broken sobs, Wheeler again managed the lopsided smile. "And it wasn't real. That's the best part, Vikki. It was illusion. All of it." He rushed on, talking around some emotion that threatened to overtake him. "I've seen their past. All of it, everything they gave up to live in this place. But it wasn't only their past I saw. It was my own as well. For the first time in my life, I've seen myself. And, for that, it was worth it. Every bit of it." The smile vanished and his voice deepened. His gray eyes fixed on hers. "There are more of them. The tombs. There must be thousands. You have to tell the Blue. Tell them to wipe these places away, clear the poison out, because it has no place here anymore."

Scuttling shadows moved closer to the fringe of light. Bloated red eyes glared at them. The mewling sounds deepened.

"We'll tell them, John," she said shakily, watching those hideous, unblinking eyes. "But we have to get out of here to do it."

"You'll need this." He reached into a pocket of his lifesuit and fished out the spud. "I shouldn't have taken it," he said, handing it across to her. "I was out of my mind at the time. I hope you understand that."

Out of his mind at the time. Right. She slipped the spud into a compartment of her belt pack and snapped it closed. "You got any idea how we can get out of here?"

He looked at her in incomprehension.

"The outer corridor," she said, holding her voice steady against the panic that was surging up inside. The shadows were drawing closer. "Stone's out there somewhere. We have to find him."

His face cleared. "Sure. I can do that." He took her light and turned suddenly to look down the passageway to their right. He nodded once to himself, muttered something she missed, and moved off down the passageway. She had no time to do anything but follow before his shambling form disappeared.

He turned in seemingly random patterns through the twisting maze. The creatures stayed clear, falling away before the bright light, regrouping behind to follow, mewling among themselves.

They walked for what seemed like a long time, and just as she had given up believing that Wheeler knew anything at all about this place, they stepped through the inner door she'd left open and she found herself once again in the short passageway that led to the outer wall and the still closed door.

"I'll need your weapon," he said. "I've run the charge out of mine."

She stared stupidly at the door. How had he known? How—?

Unidentifiable sounds came through from the other side of the wall. Stone?

"Your weapon," Wheeler repeated. He stood beside her, looking down at her. Suddenly, as she looked up at that ruined face, he seemed like the old John Wheeler: the gentle voice, the quiet patience. "Please, Vikki. I've waited a long time for this."

"You aren't leaving me here—"

Then the sound behind the door changed. She whirled around to it, felt the sizzler being plucked from her hand, and grabbed for it too late, turning back as Wheeler disappeared into the darkness. The mewling sounds rose as shadowy forms boiled forward.

*   *   *

On the other side of the wall, Stone had been busy.

Working quickly, he had released the working powerlift and reattached it near the edge of the door. The stress would not be so great there. He was counting on that to make the difference. He wound the cord tightly and knotted it around the powerlift on the opposite wall. Fractures radiated from around the locking mechanism. The wall would not hold together much longer. His hand worked the control belt, and the powerlift motor hummed, drawing the cord tight. The hum dropped to a growl as the motor strained against the solid door.

It was not going to give. Not even a tiny bit. The logistics were all wrong. The pulling force should have been opposite the door, where the damaged powerlift hung. The motor ground and popped as bearings heated with the strain. If the dead powerlift pulled out—

The door pulled free with a mind-numbing screech. The powerlift, even as it shut itself down, reeled in the sudden slack and ripped its dead companion out of the opposite wall with a crash that sent shards of broken stone flying across the corridor. The door swung back against the wall, toppled slowly, and crashed to the floor. A rumbling sound above him turned into a sudden roar.

Then he saw a flash of yellow through the swirling dust. A lifesuit—Vikki Redford, flinging herself through the opening as debris began to fall from the sagging ceiling. Stone lunged forward, grasped her outstretched arms, and yanked her into the corridor. Then they were running as the ceiling began to come down around them.

CHAPTER TWENTY-TWO

"Do you have an appointment, Mr. Clemens?"

"No, ma'am. But I have to see him right away. It's important."

"The Captain is preparing for an executive committee meeting."

"This will only take a few minutes," Lars persisted. It had taken all his courage to come here; he was not going to be put off without a fight. "Believe me, I'm not here to waste Captain Uriah's time."

"I'm sure you are not." Joseph Uriah's personal aide was an attractively mature woman with graying hair and wide-set, intelligent eyes. Even though Lars was many years her junior in both rank and age, she did not assume the condescending attitude many would have taken. "What is the nature of your business with Captain Uriah?"

"An Audit Agency crew is stranded on an undeveloped planet. I'm afraid they may be in danger, and I need Captain Uriah's help to get them back."

For the first time, a slight frown crossed her face. "You work with the Audit Agency?"

"No, ma'am. I'm with CommSec." Then, quickly: "I know what you're thinking. But it's taking too long to get this sorted out through the normal channels. I'm afraid the audit team may need help immediately. I'm hoping Captain Uriah can speed things up."

She appraised him a moment longer. "You are aware, I assume, of the position you'll be placing yourself in if the Captain disagrees with your view of the urgency."

"Yes, ma'am."

She nodded. "I'll see what I can do." She turned and disappeared through a sliding door that hissed open and closed behind her in one fluid motion. A moment later the door hissed again, and she was back. "You have five minutes, Mr. Clemens. Follow me, please."

Captain Joseph Uriah was a trim, prematurely white-haired man in his early forties. He had been given command of *Graywand* just after his thirty-ninth birthday, making him the youngest sector ship captain in Omega history and the third youngest in all of UNSA. He was already a legend on *Graywand*, with a reputation for quick thinking and a low tolerance for incompetence. Of his immediate subordinates, those who were confident about themselves and their jobs liked him, but those who occasionally fell under that scathing intolerance for incompetence feared and hated him. Although fair in his dealings, he was regarded as cool and aloof, and even those who worked close to him did not feel as if they really knew him.

"I hope this is important," he said curtly to Lars. "Maggie seems to think it is."

"Yes, sir." Lars's hands kept wanting to hold onto one another. He stood awkwardly in front of a massive desk that was made of real wood or the best substitute Lars had ever seen. Surrounding it were several plush armchairs. Uriah had not invited him to sit. "I wouldn't have bothered you with it unless—"

"I assume that."

Lars cleared his throat. "Earlier today an audit crew was stranded on a—"

"I know that," Uriah interrupted impatiently. "You do not have to repeat to me anything you've already said to Maggie. What I want to know is why you are here."

I'm wasting my time, Lars thought. He clenched his fists, felt his palms slippery with perspiration. All he was going to accomplish with Uriah was to get himself kicked out of UNSA. Going against Spick was suicidal. He should have realized that. Then he remembered McElroy's voice speaking over the commbox static, and that roaring wind in the background.

"Sir, I'm here because I'm afraid the audit crew may be in immediate danger. In my opinion we need to act quickly to get them back."

"I assume you've gone over this with Raymond Spick."

"Well—"

"I want a straight answer."

Lars felt his face grow warm. "I intended to give you one, sir. I report to Robert Spalding, Mr. Spick's assistant. I discussed the problem with him and Mr. Spick immediately after learning of it myself."

"Spick told you to keep the lid on it?"

Uriah's blunt manner once again caught Lars by surprise. He hesitated briefly before replying. "That's right, sir."

Momentary tension showed in the tightening of a muscle along Uriah's jaw. "Go on."

"Well—"

"Don't hedge with me, Clemens. I don't have the time for it, nor the patience."

"Yes, sir. I followed up on the matter myself."

"Against Spick's orders?"

"That's right, sir. I spoke to personnel in NavSec and Field Reconnaissance, and together we were able to piece together what happened and track down where the audit crew had gone."

"What was Spick's reaction to that?"

"Mr. Spick is off ship until tomorrow, sir. Mr. Spalding refuses to authorize a request to the Blue for help. He wants to discuss it with Mr. Spick before taking that step."

"A commendable attitude. After all, Spick is his immediate superior."

Lars hesitated, wondering if he had only imagined the slightly mocking tone in Uriah's voice. Uriah's eyes were steady on his own. They were the color of graymetal. Lars decided to take the plunge. "To tell you the truth, sir, I don't find Mr. Spalding's attitude at all commendable. I think his decision is a bad one, based on an inflexible and unreasonable concern for doing things by the book. A man of Mr. Spalding's experience and rank should be capable of better judgment than that."

Uriah leaned back in his chair, his face showing nothing. Behind him an old-fashioned wooden clock rang the hour. "Sit down, Mr. Clemens."

Lars sat, feeling suddenly small.

"How long have you been on *Graywand*?"

"Six months, sir."

"You came straight from the academy?"

"From the university, sir."

Uriah's eyebrows raised fractionally. "On Noura? Perhaps that explains why, with six months' experience, you feel your judgment to be superior to men who've been with *Graywand* many years."

"Captain, it seems to me—"

Uriah raised a hand. "I'm not finished. By coming directly to me you're illustrating what I find to be a disturbingly common lack of understanding of the purpose behind the organizational structure aboard *Graywand*. As with any sector ship, the structure of the management team here is a carefully designed tool of administration. It's the best way of dealing with the complex and non-routine sets of problems that make up the running of a sector ship. Decision-making activities take place at the most efficient levels, under a formal structure designed to give each layer of authority the responsibility exactly equal to its competence and experience. In short, it is designed to protect the commanding officer of a sector ship from the necessity of dealing with errors of judgment made by commclerks barely six months out of the university.''

Lars felt himself flush with anger. ''Can you be so sure from what you know about this matter that my concern is due to an error in judgment?''

Uriah's stone face remained unchanged. ''What I can be certain about goes beyond your judgment or lack thereof in this particular matter. My faith is in the administrative system that operates under me. The consequences of my interfering in this would reach far beyond any quick fix of the immediate situation. By interfering, I would be violating not only administrative order but also the confidence Spick and my other subordinates have in me and in their own levels of authority. Delegation of duties also means delegation of trust.''

Lars shook his head. ''You may be right about me, Captain Uriah. I'm inexperienced. Maybe I could have worked better with your system if I understood it better. But the simple truth is that the men who should know their way around it are using it to protect themselves rather than to get that audit crew back aboard *Graywand*.'' He stood up. ''Maybe your organization works well most of the time. But it isn't working now, and I think it's unfair to leave five people stranded on an undeveloped planet because those who should do something to help them are afraid to.''

Uriah looked up at him for a long moment. His hands were on the polished surface of the desk, palms down. ''Clemens, do you intend to make your career in UNSA?''

Lars swallowed. ''That's not important right now.''

''Yes, it is. Everything I said is true. I want to make sure you understand that, because if you don't, you do not have a place in UNSA.''

Lars shook his head, confused. ''Sir, I—''

"There's another reason I've told you all this. I want to make sure you understand that my interfering in this matter will be an extraordinary event. By doing so, I will violate many of my own pronouncements. By understanding that, you will also understand what it will personally mean to you if the facts you've given me don't stand up. Are you prepared to take that risk?"

"Of course, sir." Lars sank back down into his chair. "Does that mean you're going to help?"

"If everything you've said is true, yes. For two reasons. One, you are right in thinking that the lives of five of our auditors are more important than short-term administrative considerations. Two, the only reason my administrative system fails in situations like this is because of incompetent asses like Raymond Spick and Robert Spalding. There are still a few of them on *Graywand*. Too many, actually. They build up service years and you can't blow them out with anything less than a Kiester warhead." He smiled without humor. "Maybe this is my Kiester for Spick and Spalding." He pressed a button at the base of his commset. "Maggie, get Hans Claus. Priority. Tell him we need his help. And set up a meeting with Raymond Spick and Robert Spalding in my office at 0900 tomorrow." To Lars he said, "Mr. Clemens, you've exceeded your allotted five minutes."

CHAPTER TWENTY-THREE

When the dust settled and they saw the wreckage behind them, Stone said, "We can't go back that way. We'll have to go ahead and see if we can find another way out." A large section of the ceiling had come down when the powerlift yanked the door free, blocking the corridor with a solid mass of stone and debris. Looking at it, Stone exhaled forcefully. "You're sure about John?"

Vikki nodded without speaking. She had seen Wheeler fall under the surge of gray. She sensed the weight of the spud in the compartment of her utility belt and felt sick.

"All right." For a moment longer they stood there while the silence lay thickly around them and the darkness, curling about the cold beams of light, took on new meaning. Neither of them expected to get out of the tomb alive.

With a slight shrug, Stone turned to lead the way down the narrow corridor. After a moment, Vikki followed.

The floor curved noticeably downward here, and the gray walls revealed ancient signs of stress ranging from hairline fractures to gaping fissures. Earthquake or foundation fault, Stone guessed, or perhaps nothing more violent than the gradual shifting of great weight in key points of stress. The beginning of the end; the massive ruin was breaking apart.

They stepped across a gaping crack and began to move more cautiously as the deterioration around them worsened. Entire sections of wall had broken away, scattering debris across the floor and tearing open crypts to reveal contents which Stone and Vikki did not stop to examine. Finally, they reached a place where the floor had split into a gaping chasm.

Tom glanced at Vikki, then stepped to the crumbling edge. The chasm was wide—thirty meters, he estimated—and so deep that only on high intensity did the beam of his lantern reveal shattered boulders far below. Flashing the light across he saw, at a level slightly below the floor on which they stood, a vast, high-ceilinged chamber. The corridor had once led into the chamber, until the shifting foundation had pulled open the floor to leave the gaping crevice.

"We can't get across," Vikki said behind him. "It's too far."

He turned to look at her. She leaned against the gray wall, staring across the chasm.

"We can't get across," she said again. Her eyes moved slowly to his. "And we can't go back."

Stone flashed the beam of light along the edge of the fault. The corridor floor had formed a lip here, the wall of the crevice receding back under it, dropping two hundred meters or more to the smashed boulders and rock debris at the bottom. Broken reinforcement rods jutted out from its rough surface. Climbing down this side and up the other was out of the question; even an experienced climber would have had trouble with that shattered wall. He turned his attention to the chamber across from him. Spires, stone carvings, and webs not unlike those they had seen in the ruins of the city rose up from the floor and clung to the high ceiling. The walls were deeply etched with figures, covered with protuberances and narrow ledges. Directly across from him, the corridor continued out the other side of the chamber. Stone narrowed his eyes, training the powerful beam of his lantern along that corridor. At its furthest point, a stone stairway led upwards into blackness.

"Douse your light," he said suddenly.

Redford stared at him. "Are you crazy?"

"Just for a minute." Stone switched off his light and reached for hers. She slapped his hand away.

"*I'll* do it," she snapped.

Still she hesitated, looking around uneasily. Then she muttered a curse and switched off the powerful beam.

Stone waited for his eyes to adjust to the darkness. "There," he said suddenly. "Out in the corridor. See it?"

"How do you expect me to see anything when—" Then she stopped. They stood in the darkness listening to each other's breathing. "Stone, is that what I think it is?"

Far down the corridor across the chasm a dim glow washed over the top few steps of the stairway. Sunlight.

"It's the main entrance," Stone said, his voice rising in excitement. "That chamber was the lobby, I'll bet. Those steps lead to the outside. I'd stake my last bottle of brandewine on it."

"That isn't much help," Vikki pointed out as they switched their lights back on, "if we can't get over there."

It was, Stone had to admit, a valid observation. He studied once again the crumbling lip of stone, the black abyss; he swung his light across to the chamber floor. One step at a time, that was the key. If they let the impossibilities of it overwhelm them, they were finished.

"Check your pack," he said abruptly. "Get out your powerlifts." Shrugging the straps over his shoulders, he lowered his own pack to the gritty floor and began rummaging through it while Vikki muttered something under her breath and did the same. He popped the safety harness out of its container, worked it awkwardly over his shoulders, and pulled the straps tight to buckle them at chest, midsection, and crotch.

"Here." She handed him a powerlift pack.

"You only have one?"

"That's right, Stone. I only had two to begin with. We left one back there at the shaft. Two minus one equals one."

Frowning, he stepped to the jutting lip of stone and eyed the span to the chamber floor below. The powerlift cord was thirty meters. It would be very close.

"You aren't thinking of—?" Vikki stopped. She knew perfectly well what he was going to do. "You can't make it, Tom. There has to be a better way."

"Sure. Tell you what, you think up some better way while I set this one up. If you come up with something before I get done, let me know." He stepped away from the edge to study the distance, then returned reluctantly to the crumbling lip. It would have to be this way; there could be no margin for safety. He tested the floor with a booted heel and felt the stone shift under him. Moving along the edge, he tried again, and kept trying until he found a spot that seemed more solid than the others. He looked once again at the chamber floor.

Quiet, he said to the doubting voice inside him. *You don't have to tell me it won't be easy. I can see that for myself.*

Working briskly, he knelt and pressed the base of the powerlift against the gritty floor, holding it firm as the shafts were sunk and the pins locked into place. He gave it a tentative tug, and the base moved slightly. The motor whirred briefly, resetting the steel pins. Not good. Another tug brought the same result. Tiny fractures radiated from the base, merging into larger cracks farther out. It wouldn't take much to send this entire section down into the crevice. He drew out two meters of cord and clipped the end to his harness, then turned to Vikki.

"Have you come up with anything?"

She glared at him.

He nodded. "Plant yourself here." He tapped the powerlift with his toe. "Hold it as steady as you can."

Without another word, he turned and put his back to the chasm, lowered himself to his belly, and began inching out over the edge as stones broke loose and tumbled past him into the depths below. Vikki stepped forward and placed her boots squarely on the trembling base of the powerlift as the cord began reeling out.

With his hand at the belt control, Stone let himself slowly down along the vertical facing of stone, turning frequently to study the chamber floor illuminated by Vikki's light. The wall receded as he dropped, leaving him to swing in space, uncomfortably aware of the thin cord and the powerlift above fighting to hold onto the crumbling lip of stone. He did not look at the blackness below.

The reel ran out of cord with a jerk that made his mouth go dry. He hung at the end of its length, clinging to it with both hands while the spurt of adrenaline coursed through him like ice and his heart trip-hammered in his chest. He wanted the wall at his side, wanted to be able to reach out and touch something solid. Just when he had begun to breathe more evenly, the cord lurched convulsively.

"Tom." Vikki's voice was high and wavery. "It's coming loose. You'll have to pull yourself back up."

He hung for a moment without moving, feeling through his hands the vibration of the powerlift as it fought for purchase in the crumbling rock. Then he looked across at the chamber and nearly lost hope. Even if he could get enough arc in his swing, which was doubtful, and even if the powerlift held long enough to get that arc, which was even more doubtful, he would not be able to make it across to the floor of the chamber. The cord was simply too short.

One step at a time, he reminded himself. *First the arc. Save the worry about the rest of it until after that's been taken care of.*

Reaching up with one arm, he grasped the cord with his bare hand, gave it a half twist to tighten his grip, and pulled with an effort that produced an involuntary grunt and a few inches of slack. He reached with his other hand to disconnect the cord from the safety harness.

Don't get jittery, he said to that inner voice. *Don't think about how far it is down to those boulders.*

"What are you doing down there?" Vikki's voice was strung with tension.

"Calisthenics," Stone replied. Working awkwardly with one hand, sweating with the strain on his outstretched arm, he attached the end of the cord to itself to make a loop, then eased himself down to it while the powerlift jumped and rattled above him.

One step at a time. Just one step. But it was difficult to keep from thinking of that next step, of what would happen when the powerlift was given even more strain.

Breathing hard, he grasped the loop with both hands and hung in blackness, waiting for his heart to catch up with itself. After a moment he began to kick his legs.

Easy, he told himself. *Only enough to get the motion started.* He swung slowly out at the end of the cord, then back toward the wall. Out again, farther this time into the cone of Vikki's light. Back into darkness, then out into the light, picking up speed, clinging to the thin loop of cord. The arc widened.

"It's slipping!" Vikki yelled.

He could feel it: the sudden jerk as the cord reached the end of its outward swing and the powerlift pulled against the crumbling stone. The arc carried him back, far enough this time to brush the craggy surface of the wall. He hung there for a frozen moment, then fell back into the light, building up speed as the blackness sucked at him and the loop bit into the soft flesh of his hands. He held it tightly, oblivious to the pain, certain the jerking powerlift would break free any moment and send him plunging into the blackness below. But somehow it held as he swung up into the far side of the arc, slowly losing momentum. The cord slipped again, nearly pulling the loop out of his hands as his legs flailed for the edge of the chamber floor.

He missed, and fell back into the darkness knowing that the powerlift would never hold for another swing. He wanted to shout for Vikki to get back, to save herself and run for it, because when the powerlift pulled free, it would take a good-size chunk of the floor with it, and Vikki too if she were standing there like a fool. But his lips were tightly compressed and his mouth was dry and stuck together, and there was no way he could open it to issue that command.

By some miracle the powerlift held as he swung back through darkness, then up the side of the arc to the shattered wall. He kicked back. His feet connected solidly with rough stone and propelled him forward.

Here we go—

The cord slipped again as his full weight passed the bottom of the swing, then he was climbing through the arc, closer to the chamber floor than before, rising swiftly through the bright light, warm air brushing his face, his arms stretched above him. At the last moment he kicked out wildly, using every ounce of strength to thrust himself closer to that craggy shelf of stone.

Now.

He opened his hands and released the loop, flinging himself through the air.

It was a good solid try, but it was not enough.

Even as he released the cord and launched himself toward the jutting lip of stone, he knew he did not have enough lift to make it. The ledge fell away before his flailing arms and the abyss wheeled below. The vertical wall rushed at him. Behind him, he heard Vikki scream.

Oliver McElroy flattened himself against the wall and held his breath, giving all his concentration to the alien sounds coming from the darkness ahead. His ankle throbbed painfully, shot through with needles of a greater agony. Since losing his lantern, he'd traveled what seemed to be a good distance through the myriad corridors, groping his way along the rough walls toward the nearest of the signals picked up by his sounder. He no longer knew nor cared whose signal he was following. He was barely aware of why he was even here. He wanted only to find another human being with a light. A person could go crazy in here with those sounds all around and the darkness so thick and solid and no way of knowing what lay ahead.

He shook his head. He would not give in to panic. He couldn't.

Mewling sounds came from an adjoining corridor. They were nearby—close enough to make sweat pop out on his forehead—but not directly ahead.

He began to ease forward, trailing one hand along the wall for guidance. Getting past the creatures without being detected was a risk he had to take. The part of him that was still keeping track of such things told him he did not have time for another detour. He had already been forced to backtrack several times, taking lengthy side trips to bypass groups of the creatures. Twice he had been close to one of the pulsing signals on his shoulder, but both times had been forced to double back and approach from a new direction. All that had taken time. More time than he had to spare if he expected any chance at all of getting the spud hooked into *jack-a-dandy*'s drive system before the engines reached critical term.

He inched past the connecting passageway, holding his breath as the fetid odor washed over him. He was several meters beyond the connection when he stopped suddenly, blinking.

Far ahead was a gleam of light. Daylight, if his aching eyes were any judge.

He closed his mouth against the shout of sheer relief that struggled to get out. Daylight. He closed his eyes, held his breath, and when he opened them it was still there. Daylight. A return from the depths of blackness. A return to life.

More importantly, a way out of this place. And he was not far from that single remaining sounder. He glanced at the lighted dial of his chronometer. Forty-five minutes remained. If the blip on his sounder were Wheeler, if he could retrieve the spud and get back to *jack-a-dandy* before those forty-five minutes were up—if he could do these things, they still had a chance.

New hope surged through him as he hurried forward, his throbbing ankle forgotten. He was drawn by the pool of light, barely able to resist the impulse to run to it. It would not do to fall over something and break a leg, not with a way out of this place in sight and at least the possibility that the spud was within reach. The light brightened, growing in front of him, splashing across the corridor floor from an intersecting passageway. He came to a stop, blinking against the glare. There, to his right, a stone stairway led upwards into sunshine. He swallowed, his throat dry, legs weak and trembling with relief. The world outside—free of gray spidery things and eternal darkness and Cracchiolo's dead, faceless body.

He looked down at the sounder on his wrist. The colored lines fluttered wildly, arcing to the left. The signal was nearby, just down the corridor. With the light washing out behind him, he began running toward the signal.

There, just ahead, another light—

He tripped over a broken piece of floor and went sprawling, gathered himself up, and began running again toward that bright point. Someone was there.

The corridor widened suddenly into a vast chamber. The floor was rough and uneven, a webbed mosaic of broken boulders. Above him the ceiling sagged dangerously. A wide crack separated the floor of the chamber from the corridor beyond. On the other side of that black chasm Vikki Redford crouched, staring across at him.

CHAPTER TWENTY-FOUR

McElroy lay on his stomach and looked down over the sheer drop. Tom Stone hung against the vertical wall five meters below, snagged by a broken reinforcing rod. At first McElroy thought the rod had impaled Stone's shoulder, then saw that it had caught on one of the harness safety straps.

McElroy pushed himself back from the crumbling edge and looked across at Vikki. "Is he still alive?"

"I don't know." Her voice, echoing across the chasm, was tight and strained, the words spoken quickly and clipped off at the ends. "He hasn't moved since he hit."

Just as well, McElroy thought. If Stone even twitched he would most likely pull himself free of the rod and fall into the chasm below. There would be no getting him out of there.

McElroy went to work.

Five minutes later he had found a relatively solid spot on the floor, well back from the edge, and attached his powerlift. He gave it a tug—it was not as solid as he would have liked, but it would have to do—and clipped the end of the cord to his harness. Without giving himself time for second thoughts, he eased himself over the edge and, with one hand at the belt control and the other guiding him over rough outcroppings of stone and twisted ends of broken reinforcing rods, began a slow descent.

He had not gone even halfway when he heard a rumble above and looked up as a head-size boulder broke loose from the ledge. He hugged the wall as it cleared his left shoulder by an inch, fell through a long moment of silence, and smashed far below. Pebbles and grainy dust pattered his neck in its wake. He held his breath, waited until it was over, then fingered the control and continued on his way, keeping the powerlift motor at its lowest speed. When he'd reached a point parallel with Stone, he used his hands and knees to walk sideways to the motionless body. Stone hung limply in his harness, his face against the rough wall. A rivulet of blood ran from one corner of his mouth and down his neck, soaking into the collar of his lifesuit. McElroy could detect no sign of life.

"Tom?"

No response. He did not dare touch Stone, not with him hanging so precariously from those few millimeters of reinforcing rod.

"You'll need help over there, McElroy."

He twisted in his harness and looked up. Redford crouched on her hands and knees at the edge of the chasm, looking down at him. In the backwash of light, her face was strangely white. "I'm coming over."

"What—?"

"I'm coming over." She pushed herself back from the edge and began doing something with her belt.

"No you're not. You're staying there."

"Sure, McElroy. You betcha." Her voice quivered. McElroy realized with a shock that she was near tears. "You and Stone are going up that cord, right?"

"That's right."

"That's crap, and you know it. You don't stand a chance. There's no way the powerlift will hold both of you. It's barely holding you alone."

"I'll send Stone up first. It'll take one of us at a time."

She laughed harshly. "That's brilliant. I can see why you've reached the pinnacle of success at UNSA, McElroy. You fit right in with the jackasses that got us here in the first place. If you manage to get Stone up the wall, who's going to unhook the cord so you can bring it back down? Did you think of that? Did you give a thought to what would happen once you got him up there?" She was reeling in the cord now; he could hear the whir of the powerlift motor and the swishing sound of the cord dragging across rock. Then she stepped back out of sight—looking, he knew, for a better place to implant the powerlift. But it was hopeless. She would fail for the same reason Stone had failed. The cord was too short. He had to make her understand that.

"Forget it, Vikki. You'll never make it. Find Wheeler and get out of here."

"We found him," she shouted. "He's dead. And I can't get out of here any other way because the corridor's blocked behind me. Now, shut up. For once just try to keep your mouth shut and let me get this done."

Before he could say more, the cord above him gave a sudden lurch. He pressed himself against the stone, feeling the vibration as the powerlift sought better purchase. It couldn't hold much longer. Especially not when Vikki smashed into the wall, which was inevitable because she would never be able to reach the chamber floor above him.

Then he looked up and saw her doing a strange thing. She was peeling off her lifesuit, skinning it down over her hips, stretching the fabric over her boots to stand naked in the backwash of light. She bent to retrieve the utility belt from the corridor floor, pulled it around her bare midsection and fastened the clasps.

She's gone nuts, he thought. It did not surprise him, not after what they had been through. Then he saw her tying

one of the lifesuit's legs to the end of the cord and realized
with a sudden chill what she was going to do. She worked
quickly with the cord, her hands trembling so that she had
to make several tries at tying the knot before she got it.
Then she got down on her hands and knees and crawled
backwards over the edge, moving carefully on bare knees
over the shattered surface, shaking violently as she fumbled with the belt control. She got it set at last, and the
cord reeled out with a discernible whir.

Too fast. The crumbling floor would never take the
strain. She got her hand on the control knob and steadied
her jumping nerves enough to slow it gradually. She came
to the end of the reel; the strain was only enough to make
the powerlift jump erratically as the loosened pins sought a
better grip. The lifesuit was stretched taut; she clung to
one arm, looking across at McElroy with round eyes.

Then she swallowed—McElroy heard the dry rasp of
it—and began swinging her legs to begin her arc. The
powerlift clattered and snapped. McElroy could see the
jumping of the cord as it jerked hard enough to send
Vikki's hands slipping down the tautly stretched lifesuit.
But she hung on, kicking out to increase the arc, eyes fixed
on the chamber floor above McElroy. She swung away from
the dark wall, then came back, climbing the arc above him
far enough to nearly reach the floor, and he thought, *Let
go and try for it,* sure that it would be her only chance. For
a frozen moment she was poised at the end of the swing,
then she fell back toward the wall, and he realized she
would not have made it after all.

Again she swung back into the darkness, the powerlift
groaning and snapping above her. Small stones tumbled
past her from the floor above. Ignoring them, she kicked
hard against the wall. Then she swung out over the chasm
again, rising into the bright light, faster this time, sweeping up past McElroy toward the ledge above. She released
the lifesuit and hurtled through the air. McElroy hugged
the wall as the powerlift across from him pulled loose and
tumbled over the edge, carrying with it a large section of

the stone floor in a shuddering roar. White dust drifted across the chasm.

Then he heard a sound and looked up. Vikki peered down at him from the floor above. Blood glistened on one cheek, stark against the white patina of dust.

"You taking a break or something?" she yelled. "Get him hooked up!"

She'd made it. It took a moment to sink in. "You okay?"

"McElroy, I have never felt better in my life. The day has been just beautiful, something I'll always treasure. Now, will you please get Stone hooked up so we can get out of here?"

He looked up at her a moment longer, then turned to study the rock face around him, looking for something to hold onto. Most of the reinforcing rods had broken flush with the wall, but a few remained. The one that caught his attention protruded perhaps two inches from the wall just below Stone. It wasn't much as toeholds go, but there was nothing else to use, so he wasted no time fretting over it. Working the powerlift control with a gentle touch, he began feeling his way down and across the wall under a hailstorm of dust and small rocks. He remembered the large fractures he'd seen in the floor above Stone and thought of the cord raking across them, loosening boulders. More stones fell. He moved slowly, ducking his head as they tumbled past.

He was under Stone, reaching for that protruding finger of steel with his left foot, twisting to bring himself flush against the wall, when he heard the rumble of shifting rock and felt the cord give. He pressed hard against the wall, hoping for a miracle. But the boulder came straight down as he'd expected, dealt Stone's pack a glancing blow and tumbled past inches from McElroy's bowed head.

He lunged, somehow got his toe on the slender rod and braced himself against it to take the weight as Stone's body broke free. The powerlift cord slipped, held for a moment, then slipped again as the machine fought for a hold in the disintegrating floor. McElroy pressed himself against Stone's back, wedging his foot against the metal rod, fanning his hands out across the rock face in a futile search for something solid to hold on to. Boulders hurtled past to crash far below. He heard Vikki call out, but he ignored her; all his attention was focused on the metal rod under his toe, on the taut cord, on the rough rock against his cheek, and on Stone's weight sagging against him.

The rumble above stopped. He drew a ragged breath and held it, waiting. When no more stones fell, he risked a glance upward. Several large boulders lay exposed and loose at the edge of the chasm directly above. The powerlift cord lay between two of them. Vikki looked down from more solid ground. "What can I do?"

McElroy moved his head in a brief negative gesture, not trusting himself even to speak. By gradual degrees he shifted his weight and somehow managed to hook an arm through Stone's harness. Slowly he gave the rod under his foot his weight and faith until he felt the cord go slack. He unhooked the cord from his belt and slowly worked it around Stone's midsection to latch it over the harness.

"I'll take the controls," Vikki said. "Hold on."

Precious little to hold on to, McElroy thought.

The cord rustled as the slack was taken up, then he felt a tug and the slight easing of Stone's weight. He pressed himself against the wall, not daring even to look up as Stone was pulled slowly away. Boulders hurtled past, glanced off the wall, and crashed far below.

An eternity passed. Then: "I've got him."

McElroy looked up as Stone's body slid over the shattered edge with Vikki's hands helping it along. His toe slipped a fraction of an inch toward the end of the rod, and he pressed himself even more tightly against the wall. The rod was bending now, slowly giving way under his weight. More rocks fell.

"I'm moving the powerlift to a better spot," Vikki called. "Stone's alive, I think."

McElroy kept silent. His toe slipped again. The rod

would not support him much longer. From above came the snap of the powerlift, then Vikki's voice.

"Here it comes. Don't screw this up, McElroy. It's a long way down."

The cord snaked down toward him. Moving an inch at a time, he slid one hand across the rough stone to guide it down. His toe slipped again as he fumbled the cord's fastener, unable to open it with fingers that felt numb and awkward. He drew a breath, tried again, and succeeded in getting it hooked through his belt just as the rod under him snapped. He dropped six inches, then came to a jarring stop at the end of the cord. The powerlift jumped, then caught and held steady. He heard Vikki curse above him, then felt tension on the cord.

"I'm bringing you up. Don't let yourself get snagged on anything."

I'll do my best, he thought a little giddily. The cord pulled, jerked, stopped with an abruptness that made his mouth go dry, then pulled again. All his senses were alert, conscious of the black depths below as he walked up the fractured wall with his hands and toes, keeping the straps of his harness well away from protuberances. Then suddenly he felt that he might make it. The edge of the floor was just above him; he could almost reach it with his outstretched fingers. But the boulders were moving just above his head, pulling away from one another.

Then he was over the edge, clinging to the shifting stones, aided by Vikki's surprisingly strong hands as he scrambled away from the edge on his hands and knees while boulders slid away behind him and crashed far below.

They stood without speaking for a long time. Vikki was scratched and bleeding in a dozen places from her tumbling fall across the chamber floor. She held the spud in one hand, looking at it with a mixture of awe and disgust. "It wasn't worth it, McElroy. Not by a long shot."

"You're right."

The tone of his voice made her look at him sharply. "What's that supposed to mean?"

She didn't know about the drive engines, he realized. She and Stone had left the pod to go after Wheeler before the message came across the readout screen.

"We have the spud," she said, her voice rising. "That's all we needed. Now we can get out of here." Her eyes narrowed. "Right?"

"An hour ago we could have. It's too late now." In a few brief sentences he told her about the drive system imbalance caused by the missing spud, and of the engines building power for a blast that would wipe out everything around them. "The drive system reached critical term fifteen minutes ago."

At first, watching her features puff up, he thought she would explode. Then her face sagged in a kind of fatalistic calm. "There's nothing we can do?"

He shrugged. "We could run for it. We've got maybe two hours."

"Could we get far enough?"

"No."

Another pause. "Maybe they've come from *Graywand*."

"Yeah, maybe. Let's take a look at Tom."

Stone was still alive, which was more than McElroy had expected. His jaw was swollen and turning black, probably fractured. One arm was obviously broken, and McElroy would have bet on a few side orders of loosened teeth and cracked ribs. Not as bad as it might have been, but bad enough to keep him in bed a few days.

Then he caught himself. *In bed a few days. That's funny*.

But he did not feel like laughing.

CHAPTER TWENTY-FIVE

It took over an hour to get Stone back to the pod.

They had brought him to semiconsciousness with stimulants from McElroy's medikit, but getting him up that long stairway and across the desert floor under the blistering sun, with the wind kicking sand at them, had still required a considerable effort. They had not even discussed the alternative of staying inside the tomb. Neither of them wanted to be inside that place when *jack-a-dandy*'s engines blew. By the time they had made Stone as comfortable as possible on the cargo mat in the shade of the ledge and climbed up to the pod, they were both exhausted.

Vikki zipped up her jumpsuit and collapsed into the swivel chair. Her face glistened with sweat. "How much longer?"

McElroy shrugged. "A few minutes. Time for a cup of jo. Want one?"

"Sure."

He went to the dispenser without hurrying, banged it twice, and drew two cups. "Spice?"

She shook her head, not looking at him. McElroy handed the cup to her, then settled into the control chair. Outside, the sun burned across the desert, sinking at last toward the horizon. A gust of wind buffeted the craft. Wheeler had been right, McElroy told himself; with the temperature dropping, the wind was picking up. Not that it mattered. They sat in silence, sipping their jo while the minutes ticked by. McElroy felt the need to say something, to make a final statement of wisdom in these last few minutes. But when nothing came readily to mind, he dismissed the idea. He had heard that people often accepted death quietly, drawing on a reserve of peace inside themselves that absorbed the shock, and allowed them to approach death with a kind of majestic dignity. McElroy did not feel at all peaceful. He felt cheated. And angry. He felt the great weight of loss, for all the years that were being so casually stolen from him. He felt frustrated and helpless, but he sat quietly and kept it all inside because it would do no good to rant and rave. He would accept death quietly, but he could not accept it with inner peace.

His eyes kept wanting to move to the chronometer. But there was no future in that, so instead he reached forward to activate the console. *Jack-a-dandy* responded instantly:

R-WAVE RELAY SYSTEM EQUILIBRIUM REACHED
MR-40 FIELD EQUALIZATION WILL RESULT AT
00:08:30
00:08:29

"No!" he had not wanted it as stark as that. He wanted to get away from it; he did not want to be told so bluntly that in eight minutes he and Vikki and Tom would die.

00:07:56
00:07:55

With a savage jab, he deactivated the readout screen. Then he leaned back in the control chair, the anger draining out of him as quickly as it had come. He sipped the jo. Still half a cup left. *Better hurry it along, McElroy*. He drew a breath and let it out. He looked across at Vikki and found her watching him. She held his gaze for a moment, then let her eyes drop. This wasn't working so well, McElroy told himself. Maybe they should have run for it. They could not possibly have gotten far enough away to do any good, but running at least would have been a form of action, a protest of sorts.

The commbox buzzed.

Hot jo slopped out over McElroy's hand. His eyes jerked around to the commbox. The green light pulsed and the unit buzzed again. Incoming message.

"What the—?" He banged his cup down, leaned across the console, and flipped the switch. "McElroy here. Who's this?"

"Mr. McElroy, this is Lars Clemens on *Graywand*. I've been trying to contact you for quite some time, sir. Is everything all right there?"

The question stunned him. "No, everything is not all right," he roared. "Two of my people are dead. What's happening there?"

Commbox static filled a moment's hesitation. "I'm sorry to hear that, sir. The Blue are on their way. You've broken out on a planet called Tartarus. There was an error in the navigator's coordinates."

"Never mind that," McElroy barked. He was half standing now, leaning across the console to shout directly into the commbox. Vikki stood beside him, gripping his arm. "How soon will the Blue get here?"

"They're going through final prep now." Clemens seemed confused by McElroy's outburst. "Breakout is scheduled in just over ten minutes."

"We do not have ten minutes!" McElroy jabbed viciously at the control pad. The readout screen came to life:

00:04:20

00:04:19

"The drive engines are going to blow in four minutes," he shouted into the commbox. *"Four minutes!"*

Another brief pause. "Mr. McElroy, I don't under—"

"You do not have to understand. We don't have time for conversation right now. Just, for God's sake, get those Blue out here to pick us up *now*."

Clemens's breathing came through the commbox static. "I can't, sir. There's no way. Just no way. The cycle's opening up in ten minutes—no, eight minutes now. It's already fixed in place. There's nothing we can do to speed it up."

"What?" McElroy caught himself. Calmly, calmly. "Mr. Clemens, we are going to die if we don't get out of here in the next four minutes. Can't you bend your rules just a bit?"

"Of course, sir, if we could." Clemens spoke as if he were in pain. "But it isn't that. It's the physics of the stream. The cycle's coming around in its own time. There's no way for us to speed it up."

McElroy sank back into his chair. His eyes flicked to the readout screen.

00:03:37
00:03:36

It wasn't fair. Having it work out this way, just a few minutes short. That was all they needed, a few minutes making the difference between living and dying. It wasn't fair at all.

"Mr. McElroy?"

"Yes, Mr. Clemens."

Pause. "I'm sorry this happened, sir."

"So am I, Mr. Clemens. McElroy out." He switched off the commbox and looked at the readout screen.

00:03:00
00:02:59

Three minutes.

"So that's it," Vikki said.

He nodded without speaking. On the starboard screen

the sun was at last sinking toward the horizon. It wasn't really such a bad place, he decided, looking up at it. A bit on the arid side, but the climate techs could fix that. With a little work, the planet would be self-supporting, one of the few in Omega. Yes, a real gem. He wondered if UNSA would erect a monument here. *On this spot, five gallant auditors met their deaths while serving UNSA and humankind.*

All on their own, his eyes moved once again to the readout screen.

00:02:36

00:02:35

00:02:34

Good old *jack-a-dandy*, holding true to the end. Counting down its last few seconds—

Then McElroy sat up straighter, his eyes snapping back to the readout screen.

Realization came slowly, pulling aside by degree the shroud of defeat that had settled over him. But when it came, it did so with explosive force. He whirled around to a startled Vikki Redford. "The spud," he yelled. "Where is it? *Where is it?*" *Dear God, had she brought it back with her or had she left it there in the tomb?*

"In my belt, I think—"

"*Get it!*" He jabbed brutally at the console switch and began keying in commands.

"What—?"

"Get the spud!" he roared.

00:02:02

00:02:01

He should have thought of it before. With the spud, the drive system was operable. The engines would tear themselves and everything around them into disconnected atoms in something less than two minutes. There was no way to stop that. But between now and that two-minute deadline, the engines were operable.

00:01:56

That was the key. The engines were still operable. It was so incredibly simple. They couldn't get away from the pod, but they could get the pod away from them. With the drive system functioning, they could send the pod out into space. No matter where, as long as it was far away when it blew itself to pieces. Yes, it was all so simple—so simple he had overlooked it, and now it was probably too late.

"I've got it."

McElroy spun around, snatched the spud from a bewildered Vikki Redford, and in one fluid motion flung himself out of the chair and under the console to snap it into place. He plugged in Cracchiolo's new circuit and scrambled out. "Get out of here," he bellowed. "Take Stone and get away from the pod."

00:01:43
00:01:42

His fingers flew over the keys. There was no time to figure out coordinates. He keyed in a random set of numbers. "Get out of here," he yelled to an incomprehending Vikki Redford. "Now!" He garbled a command and had to do it over. He forced himself to concentrate, to get it right this time because there was no time to do it twice.

DRIVE SYSTEM CHECK
READY . . .

There was a command for what he wanted to do. What was it?

DELAY SYSTEM ACTIVATION

He paused sweating. How did you say one minute? He keyed:

> 00:01:00
> READY ...

He was aware of movement behind him. Vikki had come to life. He heard her step out through the hatchway and make her way down over the rocky ledge.

It was going to be okay, he thought, feeling light-headed. He would send *jack-a-dandy* out into empty space and let it turn into a miniature star all by itself. The Blue was on the way to pick them up. It would be okay. The prospect of continuing life, after death had seemed so inevitable, was incredibly sweet.

> FIX KS COMM/ENG COORSINATES
> WHAT?

McElroy stared at the brief response, frozen in momentary shock. Then he saw the error he'd made. A tiny, tiny error. His fingers trembled. He forced them to go over the keys again. There was no time for another of those tiny errors. No time.

> FIX KS COMM/ENG COORDINATES
> READY ...

Everything was set. One minute delay, then *jack-a-dandy* would skip to god-knew-where the random set of coordinates would take it, but far, from here. One minute. One final check.

> MR-40 FIELD EQUALIZATION AT
> 00:01:15

Yes, one minute was plenty of time. He almost chuckled aloud. Plenty of time by fifteen seconds. An eternity, that fifteen seconds; time to grab his log book and saunter out to join Stone and Redford, time to watch *jack-a-dandy* make its final glorious skip to oblivion.

Bon voyage, McElroy told it.

He touched the ENTER key and rose from the chair, expecting to see READY flash across the readout screen. Instead, the screen lighted with a much longer message that made his breath catch in his throat.

> FAULT—GROUND STABILIZERS
> DRIVE SYSTEM DEACTIVATED
> READY...

He stared at the screen, not breathing. Blood pulsed in his ears. He had forgotten to retract the stabilizers.

> MR-40 EQUALIZATION AT
> 00:00:58

Fifty-eight seconds.

Another gust of wind struck the pod, rattling sand against the metal skin.

> 00:00:55

Then his mind drew its second wind. Instead of going blank with despair as it might have done, it calmly analyzed the situation and informed him that fifty-eight seconds was plenty of time to retract the stabilizers and reset the skip delay. Set the delay for ten seconds, his mind said. Ten seconds was certainly enough time to get out of the pod before it skipped. If he remained calm and went through it all without screwing it up.

Thank you, mind, for remaining steady in time of stress. Oh, thank you.

He reached above the console and flicked the row of stabilizer switches with one sweep of his hand.

00:00:49

The screen flashed a new message.

NO RETRACTION STABILIZER FOUR
EXAMINE FOR OBSTRUCTION
READY . . .

The starboard stabilizer. The one they'd had trouble with earlier. It was jammed again. The useless damned thing.

Then he was out of the chair, flinging himself through the open hatchway, rolling under the pod in the burning sand. He grabbed the buckled stabilizer brace with both hands, pulled himself under it, and pushed up with all his strength. The gear moved sluggishly. He released it, brought a booted heel up and gave it a savage kick. A white-hot blade of fire sliced through his ankle as something inside pulled loose. The gear snapped up into its housing. *Jack-a-dandy* shifted slightly above him. He rolled out from under the pod, scrambled over hot sand and threw himself back through the open hatchway.

MR-40 FIELD EQUALIZATION AT
00:00:12

Sorry, his mind reported matter-of-factly. *Twelve seconds is not enough time for fancy things like delayed skips.*

He reached out, jammed his hand against the row of switches and felt the pod settle against the rock ledge as the remaining stabilizers retracted. He turned to look out through the open hatchway. Tom Stone and Vikki Redford were small figures waiting in the gathering dusk a good distance away.

Do it, McElroy, he told himself. *There's no other way.*

He swiveled back to the console and pressed the key marked ENTER.

00:00:01

There was a moment of drunk-stagger vertigo.

Vikki Redford waited beside a jagged outcropping of rock fifty meters from the pod. Stone leaned against her, barely conscious. She had known what McElroy planned to do, and she also knew instantly what had happened when she saw him explode out of the hatchway and scramble under the pod. She fully expected to be vaporized as she stood there with Stone hanging onto her and the hot wind pressing at her back.

But McElroy somehow freed the jammed stabilizer. She heard him yell out in pain, then watched as he plunged back through the hatchway and began punching at the console. When he swung around for a brief moment and looked out at her, she saw it in his face. Too late, too late . . .

Then *jack-a-dandy* was gone, and in its place was a brief flash, a pool of swirling dust, and a muted sound like distant thunder. Small stones rolled down over the ledge. A breath of warm air touched her cheek and moved on.

Three minutes later the Blue arrived.

EPILOGUE

In the months following the Tartarus incident, as the investigation blundered along in the fashion typical of any large bureaucratic machine when called upon to review its own weaknesses, the long-term veterans of Omega decided quietly among themselves that the truth about what happened on Tartarus would never be uncovered. They had seen it all before: department heads more concerned with placing blame elsewhere than with finding the truth; members of the investigating committees proceeding in a manner designed more for flattering their own careers than for finding the facts in an orderly manner; charges and countercharges traded from one agency to another, cluttering up the investigation and bringing up shields of defense so that even those with information would not readily offer it. The investigation, they knew, would flounder in its own mire, draw out until interest waned and the entire affair could be given a safe and quiet burial.

But the long-termers were wrong. They erred by not

considering the survivors of that first contact with Tartarus. Vikki Redford and Tom Stone refused to allow the investigation to drown in its own juices. With the assistance of a young commclerk named Lars Clemens and the full support of *Graywand* captain Joseph Uriah, and revealing a determination that would in later years take them both through long and successful careers with UNSA, Redford and Stone poked and prodded and kept the investigation going until the truth came out.

When the dust settled, formal action was taken against those deemed by Omega administration to be responsible for what happened on Tartarus. Robert Spalding and Raymond Spick were demoted and transferred to CommSec positions on a barren, barely habitable planet far out in the Byrn Sector. They both left UNSA after less than three months' duty at their new assignments. Jack Bannat was severely reprimanded for the clerical error which led to the duplicate set of navigation coordinates, but retained his contract and was subsequently responsible for landing twelve more ninety-nines—a record for that part of Omega. Although Gordie Turner was allotted a sizable portion of the blame for his unorthodox repair of *jack-a-dandy*'s control circuitry, he had by that time disappeared so completely into the frontier fringe at the edge of Omega that even the UNSA Internal Affairs agents could not find him.

No mention was made of faulty administrative controls in the reports that were eventually filed with UNSA headquarters on Earth. But changes were made at Omega as a result of what happened on Tartarus, and in this Vikki Redford and Tom Stone gained a small measure of satisfaction. Existing controls were reviewed and tightened, new operating procedures were developed, and administrative personnel were made to understand that complacent attitudes toward those procedures would not be tolerated. As a shock to the system, the Tartarus incident was effective. Perhaps, as some maintained, the shock was worth the price. That, too, has been debated.

Only those who died there could say for sure.

THE UNITED NATIONS SPACE ADMINISTRATION
OMEGA CENTAURI SECTOR
MOURNS THE LOSS OF
OLIVER McELROY
VITO CRACCHIOLO
and
JOHN WHEELER
WHO DIED HERE ON 32:04GCC
WHILE PERFORMING DUTIES OF THE DEEP SPACE AUDIT AGENCY

> *—Granite monument erected beneath a rock ledge just outside the perimeter of the Tartarus survey post.*